The Flying Chickens of Paradise Lane

by Sylvie Adams Hossack

Four Winds Press ✷ *New York*
Maxwell Macmillan Canada *Toronto*
Maxwell Macmillan International *New York Oxford Singapore Sydney*

Four Winds Press
Macmillan Publishing Company
866 Third Avenue
New York, NY 10022
Maxwell Macmillan Canada, Inc.
1200 Eglinton Avenue East
Suite 200
Don Mills, Ontario M3C 3N1
Macmillan Publishing Company is part of the
Maxwell Communication Group of Companies.
First edition
Printed and bound in the United States of America
10 9 8 7 6 5 4 3 2 1
The text of this book is set in Aster.
Book design by Christy Hale
Library of Congress Cataloging-in-Publication Data
Hossack, Sylvie Adams.
The flying chickens of Paradise Lane / by Sylvie Adams Hossack.
p.   cm.
Summary: As summer turns to fall on Paradise Lane, ten-year-old
Brenda Louise, her old friend McClure, and her new friend Rosie
discover that some wishes do come true.
ISBN 0-02-744565-8
[1. Friendship—Fiction.] I. Title.
PZ7.H798F1 1992
[Fic]—dc20   92-14527

For Ian
With special thanks to
Peggy King Anderson

Brenda Louise tumbled down and hit the living-room floor with a thump that rattled the vase on the coffee table.

Her brother, Tom, poked his head through the doorway. "Are you still trying to fly?" he asked. "Every time you land, you know, the whole house shakes."

Brenda Louise spun around. "I *was* flying." Anyone could see that, even her fourteen-year-old brother. Of course, she needed to learn how to stay up longer. But still, she *was* flying.

"What's all the noise? Everything all right?" Mom looked into the living room. "Brenda Louise, you weren't jumping off the couch again, were you? Look what you've done." She pointed to the couch.

Brenda Louise looked. The arms of the couch had a definite downward slant.

"The arms are squashed," Tom said. Brenda Louise glared at him.

"And the rug at the bottom of the stairs is wadded up every day. Someone could trip." Mom nodded toward the rug, hands on hips.

"The rug slides when I land," Brenda Louise said.

"I'm sure it does." Her mother sighed. "But the stairs and the couch, the whole living room, Brenda Louise, are off-limits. No more flying."

Wow!

Banned from the living room, and it was only July! Brenda Louise swallowed. Maybe she could try flying out in the yard by the garage. The grass would be softer than the floor, anyway.

Mom was watching her. Mom even had a little smile on her face. Under the circumstances, it made Brenda Louise nervous.

"Your dad and I know you've been lonely this summer," Mom said, "and we've thought of a wonderful plan, Brenda Louise. Something really special."

Special? A little fluttery feeling of danger toyed at Brenda Louise.

"There'll be plenty of kids your age," Mom continued. "You'll have lots of fun, fresh air, and exercise."

It sounded worse than anything Brenda Louise could imagine. "Mom, everything would be fine right here on Paradise Lane if there was only someone my age," she said.

"There *are* other ten-year-olds," Tom said.

"Boys don't count," Brenda Louise answered.

"Well, you still have McClure. You write to her." Tom spun his baseball cap on top of his finger.

McClure didn't count, either. Brenda Louise didn't even know where McClure was. And now Mom and Dad had cooked up some awful plan.

"Tom can have the surprise," Brenda Louise said in a sudden rush of generosity.

"No. This is just for you, Brenda Louise."

"What is it?" Brenda Louise asked, certain it wasn't anything she wanted.

"Tennis lessons," Mom said. "I've signed you up for the final session. You can use my old racket." Mom grinned at her.

Brenda Louise's heart plunged. It was worse than she'd thought. "I *hate* tennis," she said.

"There'll be children your age," Mom said. "Kimberley will be there."

Brenda Louise sighed. Kimberley was just the kind of kid who'd *like* tennis.

"I'm sure there will be other children, too," Mom added.

"Mom, I hate tennis *and* Kimberley. Summer's supposed to be fun."

"You'll like tennis, once you learn how to play." Mom patted Brenda Louise on the shoulder.

But Brenda Louise knew she wouldn't. She'd hate it. The only good thing Brenda Louise could imagine about tennis lessons was that the courts were down at the beach, and she could go swimming after class. If she forgot about tennis, summer seemed great again.

Sometimes, though, a lonely feeling swept over her like a wave on the ocean. Then her throat felt tight, and she couldn't catch her breath, as if she were really underwater.

Brenda Louise turned around and stared outside through the window so that Mom and Tom couldn't see her face. She wanted to bolt out of the room, fast, before she had to talk again.

"A long time ago, Brenda Louise, I used to play tennis with McClure's mother."

"You did?" Brenda Louise turned away from the window, trying to imagine Mom playing tennis. "It must have been a *long* time ago, Mom."

"It was the same summer you and McClure used rhubarb-leaf umbrellas in the rain."

Mom remembered that! They must have been only four or five. The gardener cut their umbrellas from the rhubarb patch at Hill House. That was when there used to be a gardener. There wasn't anyone there to take care of things now.

Brenda Louise thought about Hill House and how it looked—all empty and mysterious and overgrown. She loved to go there and look through the trees and remember how Paradise Lane used to be, before McClure moved away, before they had to write letters just to say hello.

"I've got to do something, Mom," Brenda Louise said. She ran out of the living room and up the stairs. In the hall she pulled a book off the shelf. It was the newest book McClure's parents had sent. She flipped it over. On the back of the jacket was a picture.

The caption read: "T. J. and Sam Wallingford, writer and photographer, with their daughter, McClure." McClure's mother and father smiled at the camera, looking glamorous in dark glasses, like movie stars. McClure stood in the shadows, just out of reach.

Brenda Louise stared at the picture. It could have been anybody. She stuffed the book back into the bookcase.

That night after supper, Brenda Louise crawled out of her bedroom window into the branches of the apple tree. She scrunched her eyes tight. "I want a *best* friend," she whispered.

It was powerful. Brenda Louise knew that wishes could come true—if they were made at night, outside.

"I want to fly, too," she whispered even more softly, afraid to wish for too much all at once. "I mean, *really* fly."

Brenda Louise closed her eyes again and almost fell out of the tree. She grabbed for a branch. In the darkness, she could barely see the dim outline of the garage roof. The lawn below held lots of creepy shadows. She shivered and crawled back inside.

The next week, like magic, McClure sent her a surprise. It arrived in a small box covered with stamps from an island in the South Pacific called Majuro. Brenda Louise looked it up in the atlas. On the map, Majuro was just a dot in the ocean. McClure was lucky. Brenda Louise had never lived anyplace but Paradise Lane. She tore the brown wrapper off the box and opened the lid. Inside was a handwritten note.

Dear Brenda Louise,

This is a cowrie-shell
necklace. I made it
for you.

Your friend,
McClure

The shells were white with delicate brown markings. Brenda Louise held them against her face and felt their coolness. They were satiny smooth and smelled faintly of the salt marsh at low tide. She put the shells around her neck, pretending to live on a tropical island. Getting a gift from McClure was the next best thing to having her right there.

The next day, Brenda Louise found a horseshoe crab on the beach. It was all dried out and hardly weighed anything. She put it in an old shoe box and wrapped it up to send to McClure. But before she could mail it, something wonderful happened.

Ever since she had made her wishes, Brenda Louise had gone around with an air of anticipation. She'd heard from McClure after months and months of nothing. McClure had sent a gift, even. Maybe McClure *was* still her best friend. *Anything* could happen. Today could be the first time ever for flying. *Really* flying. Her heart was ready to burst.

Inside the garage, Brenda Louise found three packing boxes. And spiders and dust. Phew. She brushed the webs away and dragged the boxes out to the driveway. There she piled them one on top of another. It was amazing how everything worked out. Three boxes all the right size—that was more than luck.

Slowly, with great concentration, she climbed to the top of the boxes. They were steeper than she'd thought, and wobbly. In fact, if she wasn't careful, she'd tip over. She held her breath at the very top and stretched her arms out for balance. All around her was blue sky. Below lay the landing place, a strip of grass alongside the driveway.

Then she jumped, shooting through the air. There were heavenly voices in the wind as she flew. Brenda Louise smiled. Nothing like that had ever happened before. Suddenly, down she crashed, the boxes tumbling around. When she stood again, gingerly, the top box lay flat beneath her. She heard the voices again.

"Smashing boxes, Brenda Louise?" There was a familiar laugh.

She whirled around and looked up into the grinning faces of Rusty Gibbons and Jimmie Scanlon, the world's worst jerks, sitting on *her* garage roof. As if they belonged there! And they'd seen her try to fly! Jimmie smirked as he leaned back against the slant of the roof.

Heavenly voices! Jimmie and Rusty were the most unheavenly people she knew. Brenda Louise swallowed. "As a matter of fact, that's exactly what I'm doing. Helping to recycle," she said. She dragged the flattened box into the garage, careful not to limp as she walked.

"We'll help," Rusty said, and then laughed.

"No, thanks." She heard them whispering, up to no good. She ran back outside. "And you better get off the roof." She glared at them.

Splat. The first water bomb hit. *Splat splat.* The flimsy plastic bags split as they smacked her on the head and shoulders, bursting, drenching her hair and shirt.

"I'll get you!" she yelled. Little rivers of cold water ran down her face and arms.

The boys jumped off the low side of the garage roof, giggling. In two leaps, they cleared the hedge and disappeared.

Brenda Louise walked back to the house and let the screen door slam. Loud.

"Mom!" she called. She grabbed a kitchen towel and dried her arms and face.

"She's not back yet," Tom shouted.

Brenda Louise stomped through the family room.

"What happened to you?" Tom asked.

"Water bombs." She wrung her hair out. "Rusty and Jimmie. From *our* garage roof."

"Couldn't you duck? You look like you practically drowned."

Brenda Louise swirled her hair, spraying Tom as she passed.

"Oh, nice job," he said.

Out back, a car door slammed.

"Mom's back," said Tom, "and you're getting the floor wet."

Mom came up the walk, carrying groceries. Brenda Louise held the screen door open.

"Brenda Louise, stop dripping water all over the floor." Mom took the bag of groceries into the kitchen.

"But, Mom, I've got to tell you what happened while you were gone. It was awful." Suddenly it all came back in a terrible rush, how she'd thought she was all alone, thought it was safe to fly. "Jimmie and Rusty were up on our garage roof. They're real rats, Mom. They threw water bombs on me."

Her mother unpacked the bag on the counter. "Please wipe the floor, Brenda Louise."

"They should be arrested or something, Mom. I mean, when a person is in her *own* yard minding her *own* business, rotten rats should stay off *her* garage roof."

Mom was smiling. Brenda Louise bet Mrs. Scanlon and Mrs. Gibbons wouldn't be smiling if Brenda Louise climbed their garage roofs and dropped water bombs.

"We should put up a fence, Mom."

Mom closed the refrigerator door. "They shouldn't be on our garage roof. And I'm sure you told them that." Mom paused as she looked at Brenda Louise.

"Yes, I told them." Brenda Louise remembered that it was *after* she told them that they dropped the water bombs. "I walked right into it, Mom. I mean, I should've *known*." She shook her head. "But the very worst part of all, Mom," Brenda Louise whispered, "is that they saw me learning to fly." She looked over at Tom. She didn't want him to hear.

"I thought it was something like that," Mom said.

Mom grabbed a towel and fluffed Brenda Louise's hair.

"Come on, I'll take you down to meet the tennis pro, Nicky. Your class starts next week."

"I don't want to, Mom! I've got enough to do around here."

The phone rang, and Mom went to answer it. Brenda Louise sat down at the table. She thought about flying that morning. There hadn't been anything different at all about the flying part. Having wishes come true took a long time.

Mom was already back, the towel in her hand. "Mrs. James is giving a party this weekend, and we're all invited."

"Do I have to go? She never has kids at her parties."

"Guess who else is coming?" Mom's eyes twinkled. "McClure's coming home. She'll be there."

3

The day McClure came back, it was sticky-hot. Not one breeze. Everyone at the Jameses' party sat in the shadows on the terrace, except Brenda Louise. She watched for McClure in front, with the sun beating down. She didn't mind. After all, McClure was going to be *her* best friend. They would fly together. Brenda Louise spun around on the grass.

Any minute—McClure and her Aunt Julia would arrive. *Any minute.* Brenda Louise shielded her eyes and scanned the road between the trees for the car. It was worse than waiting to open presents. And sometimes, Brenda Louise remembered, when you opened a present, you didn't get what you expected. Not at all.

What if McClure's coming back was like that? What if they didn't like each other after all this time! Maybe it wasn't such a good idea, being the first one to welcome McClure home.

It was too late. Brenda Louise heard the roar of a sports car. There was a flash of blue flying between the trees.

"They're here!" Brenda Louise shouted toward the terrace. She turned. Aunt Julia's car barreled down the drive in a swirl of dust. Brenda Louise jumped back. The convertible, top down, shot past her; Aunt Julia's scarf soared like a parachute. Next to Aunt Julia sat a huge brown poodle. Brenda Louise looked for McClure. But all she saw were two feet sticking out of the backseat, up in the air.

When the car stopped, Brenda Louise ran up and opened the door. Aunt Julia hopped out and hugged her.

"How you've grown. It's wonderful to see you."

Brenda Louise hugged her back, but she kept looking around Aunt Julia's shoulders at the car. The two feet disappeared, and up stood a skinny girl with blond hair. She wore a man's leather jacket.

"McClure?" Brenda Louise frowned.

"Is that you, Brenda Louise?" McClure jumped out of the car.

Brenda Louise untangled herself from Aunt Julia. "Of course, it's me."

McClure leaned against the car. "You've changed."

"No, I haven't." McClure was the one who was different. And she wore that big jacket. "Aren't you hot in that thing?" Brenda Louise asked.

"Sure. Neat isn't it? Genuine leather World War II aviator jacket. Got it in Hong Kong."

Brenda Louise was impressed. For some things, the heat didn't matter. The jacket was the kind you might see in the movies on TV. "It's nice, all right." She grinned.

"What happened to your teeth?" McClure asked.

Brenda Louise held her hand up, covering her mouth. "Nothing."

McClure laughed. "You've got braces." McClure's teeth were white and perfectly straight.

Brenda Louise didn't think it was funny at all.

McClure slipped her jacket off. "Hold this for me, will you?"

McClure was a golden color. Brenda Louise was sure her own face was blotchy red. It got that way in the heat. She reached for the jacket, and the weight pulled her arm down. Her mouth fell open with surprise. "This weighs a ton."

Brenda Louise dragged the jacket over the grass as she walked. The big poodle slipped out of the car and followed her.

"Meet Mr. Brown," McClure said. "He's my dog from France. He's learning English."

Mr. Brown tap-danced closer to Brenda Louise.

"I should warn you, he doesn't like strangers," McClure said.

Mr. Brown sniffed Brenda Louise's sandals, his nose cool on her toes. Sniff. Sniff. Brenda Louise stood very still. Mr. Brown licked her fingers.

Brenda Louise took a breath. Slow. Mr. Brown was big. She reached out; her hand sank into his fur. It felt soft. Mr. Brown let out a sigh and slouched against her leg. Trapped, she watched everybody walk up from the terrace to greet McClure and Aunt Julia.

Tom came around the corner of the house. "How ya doin', McClure?" he asked. He leaned against the car.

"Just fine," McClure answered.

Then everyone was by Aunt Julia's car, all of McClure's aunts and uncles and cousins, yelling and shouting "McClure!"

Brenda Louise still didn't move. She watched McClure run off. She wanted to run, too. Only now, Mr. Brown lay on top of her feet. She couldn't feel her toes. And she couldn't put something as special as a World War II aviator jacket just anywhere. But her arm was tired, and part of the jacket still dragged on the grass.

McClure danced in the sunlight. "Come on," she yelled. "It's almost dark. Let's play."

It was about time McClure remembered her. Still holding the jacket, Brenda Louise wriggled her feet out from under Mr. Brown. She ran.

McClure grabbed her hand. "Crack the whip," she yelled. Tom and the cousins led the way. Around and around they went, spinning. Brenda Louise went flying and landed in a heap on the ground.

"Are you okay?" McClure asked.

Brenda Louise nodded. She didn't have any breath left inside. Everybody tumbled into the pile. Soon the others ran off to play again. It was just McClure, Tom, and Brenda Louise. The three of them sat on the ground. Suddenly, it seemed cooler and darker. Brenda Louise put on McClure's leather jacket. She smelled supper cooking in the kitchen. Spaghetti sauce. Her mouth watered.

"My stomach's rumbling," McClure said. She scraped a pile of twigs and grass together as she talked. "Found one," she announced.

"Found what?" Brenda Louise asked. She leaned against Mr. Brown.

"A worm." McClure held a long, wriggling earthworm.

"It's a nice fat one. I sell worms like that to the fishermen at the lake," Tom said.

"I don't want it for fishing; I'm going to eat it." McClure held the worm high over her open mouth, her head back. No one said anything. Then she lowered her arm and looked at Brenda Louise. "I didn't mean to be rude. You can have this one. There's plenty to go around."

"I've never eaten worms," Brenda Louise said. She felt scared. What if she had to eat one—to prove herself? What if this was part of being McClure's friend!

With that, McClure plopped the worm in her mouth, swallowed, and smiled. "Not bad." She wiped her lips with the back of her hand. There was a streak of dirt on her chin. "My dad likes fried grasshoppers," McClure said. "I prefer worms." She jumped up and ran down the Jameses' hill. It was nearly dark. She climbed a maple tree and hung upside down from the bottom branch.

Brenda Louise glanced over at Tom. "Do you think she really ate that worm?" she whispered.

Tom nodded.

"I wonder what it tasted like," Brenda Louise said.

"I don't think I want to know," Tom answered.

"Dinner," came a call from the house.

McClure swung down from the tree and ran up the hill. She joined Tom and Brenda Louise as they walked inside. Every chair was taken. Brenda Louise and McClure edged into the buffet line, picking up plates.

Mrs. James stirred the sauce. "Don't be shy. We have plenty. I know you love spaghetti, Brenda Louise." With her serving tongs, she lifted a big clump of pasta down onto Brenda Louise's plate. Brenda Louise spread sauce over the top.

"Save some for the rest of us, Brenda Louise. You don't need to drown your spaghetti," Tom said.

Brenda Louise glared. She sprinkled grated Parmesan all over the sauce. Then she squeezed between two chairs, holding her plate out as she sat on the floor.

"Save me a place," McClure said. Her plate was piled high with spaghetti, too. And she had lots of sauce and cheese, just like Brenda Louise did.

Brenda Louise twirled long strands of spaghetti around her spoon. She glanced over at McClure and grinned. McClure burped. Brenda Louise took another big bite. McClure burped again. Louder. There was a chorus of burps as the cousins joined in.

"This is wonderful spaghetti, Mrs. James," McClure said. "In some places, it's polite to burp, to show you like the food."

What a great idea! Brenda Louise planned to try it sometime herself.

But Mrs. James had a strange look on her face. And Mr. James' face turned red. "Enough!" he said. No one burped again.

"When do your parents return?" Mr. James asked McClure.

"I don't know. They're on another expedition in the jungle." McClure's voice was soft. Brenda Louise could hardly hear her. "The housekeeper's going to open Hill House."

What would it be like to own several houses in different parts of the world, like McClure's parents? It would be wonderful. Brenda Louise looked at McClure with admiration.

But McClure studied the pattern in the rug. She looked tired. And sad. Maybe it wasn't always so wonderful to have famous parents and live all over the world. Maybe McClure got lonely, too.

"Did you ever eat any of that raw fish in Japan?" she asked McClure. Raw fish seemed like a McClure type of thing.

McClure nodded. Brenda Louise tried again.

"Sometimes they find worms in the fish. Once they even operated on a guy, took his appendix out. They found a two-inch worm crawling out of his stomach."

"We're eating dinner," Dad said.

"Gross, Brenda Louise." Tom shook his head. But McClure's eyes twinkled.

"I know worms from raw fish or meat are dangerous—what about earthworms?" Brenda Louise asked, frowning.

"Why do you want to know?" Dad asked.

"Just wondered." Brenda Louise stood up and carried her empty plate to the kitchen. She couldn't tell her parents McClure ate earthworms. She wanted them to let her invite McClure to spend the night.

Mom followed Brenda Louise and rinsed some plates in the sink. Brenda Louise leaned against the counter. "Mom, McClure needs a place to stay. Until Hill House is opened." Brenda Louise crossed her fingers behind her back.

"With all these relatives, McClure doesn't have a place to stay?" Mom asked.

"Please, Mom." Brenda Louise held her breath. Mom just had to say yes.

It was very late when McClure and Brenda
Louise went up to sleep. Brenda Louise
jumped onto her bed. She did that each night, just
in case. She never knew if someone had tried to
sneak under her bed and hide. Not that anyone
would fit. The space wasn't big. And they'd sneeze
from all the dust balls. But she did it just the same.

She tossed her sheet high and let it billow out
like a parachute. It floated down and covered her
up. She lay there, grinning in the dark. She felt the
cool air from the open window, heard the peepers
in the ditch outside.

McClure lay on the camp cot. She was probably tired from all that travel and the party. Even Mr. Brown acted worn out. It was okay. They were here! Brenda Louise scrunched into the softness of the mattress and looked over at McClure.

"Are you asleep?" she asked.

"Yes," McClure whispered.

"I wish you were awake."

Brenda Louise heard a low chuckle. She started to laugh, too. McClure's laughing made you laugh back. McClure leaned on her elbow and turned toward Brenda Louise's bed.

"Are you hungry?"

"It depends." With McClure, you couldn't be too careful when it came to food.

"I've got a surprise for you in my knapsack." She slipped out of bed and ran across the room. Brenda Louise flipped on her bedside lamp. McClure dragged her knapsack over. She felt inside the bag and pulled out a pair of red socks and a bathing suit. Then she felt around some more and tugged at something, inching it up. Suddenly, she held a wooden box. She handed it to Brenda Louise.

The lid had a picture of violets and roses painted on the top. It was one of those old-fashioned pictures with writing in script that curled around the flowers. Everything was written in French.

"Go ahead. Open it."

The lid came off in Brenda Louise's hand. Nestled inside rows of folded paper was a mound of fragile bits of lavender and pink. They rattled together when she shook them.

"What are they?"

"Candy. Made from rose petals and violets. The French do stuff like that. Try some." McClure sat back on the end of Brenda Louise's bed. Her eyes sparkled in the light.

Brenda Louise took a rose petal and popped it into her mouth. It was an improvement over the worm McClure had offered her that afternoon. The flavor was delicate. "Gee, McClure, this is good." She held the box so that McClure could reach it, too.

Brenda Louise took a few more pieces and leaned back against the wall. "I'm glad you're back." It felt really exotic eating rose petals and violets. "We can have lots of fun this summer." Brenda Louise crunched down on a candied violet. She was bursting to tell McClure just how much fun.

"It'll be super." McClure yawned as Mr. Brown crawled up onto the bed between them.

Then McClure stood up and lurched toward the cot. "I'm *sooo* tired." Mr. Brown followed her. He lay down on the floor with a bump. Brenda Louise moved into the warm spot he'd left on her bed and flipped off the lamp.

"Thanks for the candies."

"I thought you'd like them."

Now was the time to tell McClure about flying. Somehow it seemed easier to tell in the dark. She heard McClure slide under the sheets on the cot. She swallowed hard. "Have you ever wanted to fly?" Brenda Louise asked. "I don't mean in an airplane. I mean for real—just yourself—in the air."

McClure mumbled. Brenda Louise was sure it was a yes mumble. She remembered standing in the apple tree wishing for a best friend. Then wishing she could fly. "I think it's going to happen this summer, McClure. Flying." She snuggled under the top sheet. "You see, McClure, I've always wanted to fly. I've only done short flights so far. It's *wonderful*. There's nothing like it. You'll see." Brenda Louise stared through the darkness. "Are you asleep?" she asked.

The room was quiet except for the peepers outside and the breathing sounds of McClure and Mr. Brown. Brenda Louise wondered if McClure had heard anything she'd said.

When Brenda Louise woke up, she looked at the camp cot where McClure slept, her head buried under the pillow and her sheets draped partly on the floor. Mr. Brown lay under the cot, watching Brenda Louise.

"Bonjour, Mr. Brown," she whispered, remembering he only understood French. "Good morning." He might as well start learning some English. She paused, and then added, *"Bonne nuit."* What the heck. *Good-night* was okay, too. It wasn't as if she knew a lot of French words. And Mr. Brown didn't seem to mind. He rolled over

upside down, his paws in the air, and grinned. His white teeth sparkled.

Brenda Louise inched out of bed and crouched next to him. Mr. Brown rolled right side up and thumped his tail on the floor. "Shh." Brenda Louise looked at McClure to see if the noise had awakened her. McClure didn't move. On the back of the desk chair was the World War II genuine leather aviator jacket from Hong Kong. Brenda Louise slipped it on over her nightgown.

Mr. Brown padded after her as she tiptoed into the hall and down the stairs. It made her feel good, having Mr. Brown there.

Dad was in the kitchen, fiddling with the radio dial. "It's going to be a scorcher today," he told her.

It was already starting to get warm. Brenda Louise sat down on the back-porch steps. Mr. Brown sniffed the flowers by the edge of the field; and soon all she could see was the tip of his tail as he plowed through the tall grass.

The katydids strummed louder and louder. Dad clanged the pans together as he got breakfast.

"Where's McClure?" Mom asked Brenda Louise through the screen door.

"Sleeping."

"Won't be for long," said Tom. "Not around here." Brenda Louise could see him leaning into the screen, making it bulge.

"Better wake McClure, Brenda Louise. We'll be eating breakfast soon," Mom told her.

Brenda Louise left the porch slowly. "Mr. Brown!" The tail stopped moving. *"Monsieur Brown?"* Suddenly, the tail moved fast as Mr. Brown made a path through the field, the grass bending before him. "Come on," she told him.

At the edge of the field, Mr. Brown looked at Brenda Louise and wagged his tail. Then he ran across the lawn, bounded up the steps, and followed her inside. His fur was damp with the morning dew.

"Who let that wet animal into my clean kitchen? Brenda Louise, get that dog outside!"

The sound of Mom's voice chased them as they ran upstairs. By the time Brenda Louise and Mr. Brown reached her room, she hardly had any breath left at all. She yanked the bedroom door open. McClure sat on the floor. She looked like a yoga pretzel. Mr. Brown bounced over to her and shook his coat.

"Yikes," McClure yelled as Mr. Brown shook some more. She wiped spatters off her face. "Where've you been?"

"Outside," Brenda Louise panted. "Mr. Brown's been in the field."

"Brenda Louise!" Mom's voice sounded closer.

"It's time for breakfast—are you ready?" Brenda Louise asked.

McClure unwound herself and stood up. "Sure. Let's go."

Brenda Louise hesitated in front of McClure's sandals. They looked unusual, different. They had truck-tire soles. Brenda Louise had never seen anything so great. "McClure, you want to trade sandals? I mean for today." She talked fast, afraid McClure might say no.

"Sure, I'll trade."

"How about my jellies?"

"Neat," McClure said as she held them up.

Brenda Louise picked the truck-tire sandals up off the floor and slipped a strap on. Wow. The sandals made her tall. She bounced with each step. They looked great.

"Let's wear sunglasses, too." Brenda Louise handed McClure a pair. She put her own on and squinted into the darkness. Together they clumped out to the kitchen.

"Brenda Louise, didn't you hear me calling you?" Mom asked. She stood in the kitchen with her hands on her hips. Then she smiled. "I think you both can take your sunglasses off for breakfast."

Tom took a last big bite of pancake. His plate empty, he shoved his chair away from the table. "I'm done. I'll do the lawn now," he announced.

They watched as he leaped down the porch steps, two at a time. His baseball cap was on backward, shading his neck. He leaned over the power mower and pulled the cord. The mower roared, and Tom zoomed around the yard.

"You have chores to do, too, Brenda Louise. I want you to clean the mildew off the picnic table," Mom said. "After breakfast."

"I've got company, Mom." Brenda Louise looked at McClure.

Dad handed them each a plate of pancakes. "Then you'll have help doing your chores, Brenda Louise. We're going to have a barbecue for McClure. We'll need that table."

Brenda Louise kept quiet. She didn't want to push Mom and Dad too hard. She poured syrup onto her pancakes.

"Breakfast is delicious," McClure said as she smiled. "Blueberry pancakes are my favorite." McClure's teeth were stained purple-blue.

Mr. Brown lay under the kitchen table, his head resting on Brenda Louise's feet. She felt his fur with her toes. He was a wonderful dog. She leaned down and petted him.

That's when she noticed paw marks on the kitchen floor. She wondered if Mom had seen. She knew they needed to get out of the kitchen quickly. "We'll do a great job on that table, Mom."

She carried her dishes to the sink. "You almost done, McClure?" she asked. "I'll get the brushes and a bucket while I wait."

McClure nodded as she wiped syrup from her mouth.

"Let's go." Brenda Louise held the screen door open as McClure and Mr. Brown followed her out into the backyard.

She slopped water on the table, handed McClure a brush, took one for herself, and started scrubbing. All you could hear was the sound of bristles scratching the wood. Bits of black appeared in the soapsuds—furry pieces of mildew. Brenda Louise swirled the black into circular patterns, pretending to be very interested in the mildew hiding in deep grooves of the wood. She could never remember being so interested in mildew.

Who was she kidding? She didn't like mildew. She just didn't know how to talk to McClure. There was so much to tell her. Brenda Louise didn't know where to begin. She leaned her hand against her scrub brush. With all the scrubbing, her arms ached. Brenda Louise stretched, lifting her brush high. The soapy water with the fuzzy mildew splashed on her forehead.

"Ick!" Brenda Louise lowered her arm and wiped her face with her T-shirt. She shuddered. "I've got this awful stuff on my face."

From the other end of the table she heard a low giggle. McClure stood back from the table. Her shorts had streaks of mildew and water all over the front. "There's a fungus among us," she said.

Brenda Louise grinned. She felt like the sun suddenly turned on full power.

She tossed her brush into the bucket and surveyed the tabletop. "It looks pretty good, don't you think?"

McClure nodded and dropped her brush onto the grass. "It's an expert job," she said.

They tugged at the table, moving it into the sun to dry. The day was bright and clear, perfect for flying. Had McClure heard what she'd said last night? Brenda Louise didn't want McClure laughing, making her feel foolish.

She swallowed. "We'll go flying after lunch, if you'd like to," Brenda Louise said.

McClure looked up at Brenda Louise real fast. Her eyes narrowed. "Are you putting me on?"

"No." Brenda Louise took a deep breath. "Remember, I told you about it last night. Flying, I mean. Maybe you were sleeping." She crossed her fingers for luck. Things couldn't go wrong now. Not when everything seemed to be working out just like she'd wished.

"You mean *really* flying? Not like in a plane? How do we do it?"

"I'll show you," Brenda Louise said. "I don't have it down perfect yet, but I can teach you." Her voice trembled. She wanted McClure to believe so much.

McClure didn't say anything. Brenda Louise

looked down at the ground. Maybe it had been a mistake to tell McClure, a dreadful mistake. Her eyes started to fill with tears.

Shoot.

She looked away. Who was she kidding? No one had ever actually flown. Not the way she wanted to do. Who could blame McClure if she didn't believe it could be possible?

"I thought maybe you were kidding," McClure said. "Let's try it!"

Brenda Louise spun around. McClure and Mr. Brown stood there in the sun, watching her.

Brenda Louise did a cartwheel on the grass. "I thought you might think it was dumb." She leaped across the lawn. "After lunch! We'll go flying after lunch." Barking, Mr. Brown chased her. She heard McClure laughing as she ran to catch up.

For lunch, the family sat on benches around the picnic table. Brenda Louise's dad barbecued chicken on the grill. The yard smelled of fresh-cut grass, smoke, and pickle juice.

"Brenda Louise, I saved the wings for you," Dad said.

Tom looked at McClure and smirked. "Brenda Louise thinks they'll help her fly."

"I'd like one, too," McClure said as she leaned over the picnic table, holding her plate out. She wiggled one of her eyebrows at Brenda Louise. One eyebrow! Brenda Louise tried to wiggle one, too, to show she got the message. She decided she'd have to work on the eyebrow thing. She could feel both of hers go up together. But Mom and Dad and Tom weren't watching her eyebrows, they were watching McClure, their forks suspended over their plates. No one liked chicken wings. Brenda Louise ate them on the chance that they might help her fly. But McClure acted like it was an honor. She held the chicken wing delicately.

"Best part," McClure said. "Best flavor."

Brenda Louise gave Tom her metal-mouth grin. "It just so happens, we are going flying after lunch."

"Humph," said Tom. "Fat chance."

"Eating chicken wings has nothing to do with it," Brenda Louise continued. "If it were that easy, everybody'd be flying." She smiled mysteriously. No need to tell too much. He'd just want to fly with them. She helped herself to more potato salad and passed the bowl to McClure. The lettuce salad was already gone. Even the raw onions in it. They'd have onion breath. The whole family.

"We're finished, Mom. Can we go?" Brenda Louise scraped her plate with her fork.

Mom nodded.

"The food was great," McClure said. She reached over and took a cookie.

"Come on, McClure." Brenda Louise walked

across the lawn to the back porch, behind the garage. No one could see them there. "Your first flight'll be from here." Her hands felt clammy. She jumped up the steps. "See. It's easy."

Brenda Louise leaped off the third step and landed standing up on the grass. " 'Course, to really *fly*, you have to be higher."

She climbed to the top of the porch railing, un-did the tire sandals, and threw them to the side. Then she perched on the top rail post with her arms spread out.

"You have to balance, close your eyes, and wish real hard." Brenda Louise teetered back and forth.

She scanned the landing place. At the same time, she sneaked a look at McClure. McClure was watching her every move. For the actual flight, Brenda Louise closed her eyes and wished with all her might.

Suddenly, she *was* flying. Her stomach lurched, and she screamed as she hurtled through the air. It was a beautiful flight. Mr. Brown barked and danced around her as she landed.

"Wow," McClure said. "It looks really high."

"Aw, if I can do it, you can, too," Brenda Louise said casually, trying to hide her apprehension. She wanted McClure to like flying.

"Okay." McClure climbed up to the top post lickety-split.

All of a sudden, Brenda Louise felt that teaching McClure might be a scary adventure. After all, McClure was a girl who had eaten a worm. Brenda Louise wasn't sure McClure had any fear at all. How high would McClure want to fly?

"You better take these," McClure said, and handed Brenda Louise her sunglasses.

McClure stood on the top post like she'd been flying all her life. And then she leaped, her eyes closed tight, wild and fearless. She screamed, too, and landed with a bounce, standing on the grass. "Let's do it again!"

"Okay, come on." Brenda Louise ran to the little plum tree next to the garage. "We'll go off the garage roof."

"The *garage roof*?" McClure's eyes looked big. McClure was scared! Brenda Louise couldn't believe it.

Brenda Louise climbed the tree and hoisted herself onto the roof. Actually, the garage was so small that even Dad's little car didn't fit inside. Some people might even call it a shed.

But McClure seemed properly impressed. She climbed up the tree and stepped onto the roof behind Brenda Louise, and Mr. Brown followed her! Brenda Louise had never seen a dog climbing a tree.

McClure giggled. "I taught him." Mr. Brown

wagged his tail. He used the tree limbs like a ladder. When he got near enough to the roof itself, he hopped over.

The garage was low to the ground and the roof on this side wasn't high—not even as high as Dad. Brenda Louise liked people to think the roof was high. If you jumped off a garage roof, that was a big deal, as long as no one knew it wasn't a tall roof. Actually, from on top, it *was* taller than she remembered. But she was teaching McClure, and she couldn't be scared.

The three of them—McClure, Brenda Louise, and Mr. Brown—sat in a row and looked down. The ground was very far away. Brenda Louise stood up slowly.

"We have to hold hands when we fly from here," she told McClure. "That way, no one can chicken out."

McClure swallowed sort of fast. "We'll be the Flying Chickens," she said.

The Flying Chickens! It was *perfect.* Brenda Louise grabbed McClure's hand. "Okay." They each took a deep breath, and flew off into space. Brenda Louise's insides turned upside down. She screamed. McClure screamed. Then they landed. They lay on the ground and giggled.

But Mr. Brown was still on the roof, barking and running along the edge. They couldn't get him to jump. Finally, Brenda Louise had to run back to the picnic table and get Dad to help. He gathered up Mr. Brown in his arms. Scooped him right off the roof. Mr. Brown's body overlapped Dad's arms and his legs dangled as he wriggled and licked Dad's face.

"He's just a big baby," Dad said as he put Mr. Brown on the ground. "I want you both to be careful jumping off the roof."

"Dad, we're flying off the roof," Brenda Louise protested. "And it isn't all that high."

Dad put his hands on the edge of the roof. "Be careful just the same," he said in his no-nonsense, *you-will-listen* voice.

"Okay, Dad," Brenda Louise said. "And thanks for helping Mr. Brown."

"Mr. Brown is an honorary Flying Chicken," McClure announced.

Which wasn't bad for a dog who didn't speak English.

The next morning was Sunday. Brenda Louise leaned out of the shower and yelled to McClure.

"Want to go to church today? You can sing in the choir with me." Actually, she wasn't sure she could sneak McClure into choir. Mr. Gerald was strict. He didn't like surprises, especially on Sunday morning, just before the service. But it was worth a try. She couldn't very well leave McClure at home.

"What do you wear?" McClure asked when Brenda Louise was finished in the bathroom.

"Whatever you want. Father John says people should be comfortable, just come as they are."

Brenda Louise pulled her blue dress over her shoulders.

"I'm not used to church." McClure frowned. "But I'll go."

Mr. Brown pranced between them, playing with Brenda Louise's sandal. "You can't come this morning," she told him as she stroked his head. "But we'll be back soon. *Au revoir.* Good-bye."

Mr. Brown let out a loud sigh.

"Our ride's here," Brenda Louise yelled to McClure.

Kimberley's father always drove Brenda Louise to church. Mr. Ryan was nice, but Brenda Louise couldn't understand how he'd ended up with such a terrible daughter. As they climbed into the car, Kimberley arched her eyebrows. She sneered at McClure's jacket and tapped her patent-leather shoes impatiently. Everything about her was phony baloney. "Something smells in here," Kimberley said.

Brenda Louise felt the cowrie-shell necklace around her neck. She'd worn it to show McClure how it looked. "It smells like the salt marsh at dead-low tide," she said.

"It stinks like something died." Kimberley rolled down the window and stuck her head out.

Her father glanced at the necklace as he drove.

"Most unusual," he said. "Very pretty. It's a bit warm, don't you think?" He rolled his window down, too.

"McClure made it for me," Brenda Louise told him. "She sent it from the South Pacific."

McClure buried her face in her hands. Her whole body shook. Was she crying? Poor McClure. People didn't appreciate tropical things. Then Brenda Louise heard a muffled giggle. McClure looked at Brenda Louise.

"It does stink," McClure said. "I'm sorry, Brenda Louise. When I made the necklace, I didn't know the creatures were still inside the shells."

Brenda Louise felt the lovely coolness of the shells. "I don't care, McClure. I love this necklace."

"We can fix it, you'll see," McClure promised. "We'll bury it. The ants will do a great job. They'll eat the dead bodies. Then it won't smell any-more."

"You can leave it in the car, Brenda Louise," Mr. Ryan said. Brenda Louise put the necklace under her car seat.

"Now the car will stink," Kimberley complained.

Her father frowned. "That's enough, Kimberley."

Kimberley hurried out of the car as soon as it stopped. She held her nose.

When they got to the choir room, kids were milling around the piano. The choir director, Mr. Gerald, was leafing through sheets of music. No one seemed to notice their arrival.

Brenda Louise scanned the benches to find a good place to sit and saw Rosie sitting in the very top row with her feet propped up against the row in front, watching the room below.

"Hey, Metal Mouth, who's your friend?" Rosie asked.

When Rosie talked, it was impossible to ignore her; her voice boomed. Rosie was the only person Brenda Louise allowed to call her Metal Mouth. Of course, Rosie pretty much did whatever she wanted to, anyway.

"Rosie, meet McClure," Brenda Louise said.

Rosie leaned forward to check out McClure.

"Hi," said McClure as she slipped off her jacket. She looked up at Rosie and smiled.

Rosie jumped down the rows till she stood next to them. "That's a mighty fine jacket." She reached out and smoothed the leather with her hand.

"Try it on," offered McClure.

Rosie slipped into the jacket. "How do I look?" She turned in a circle like a model.

Kimberley leaned over from her seat. "You certainly aren't dressed appropriately for church." Her chin jutted out in the air.

Rosie snorted.

"Why, you look grand," said McClure.

"I do, don't I?" Rosie did a fast two-step and took the jacket off.

"Let's sit up here," said McClure, climbing up after Rosie. The two of them looked down at Brenda Louise from the top bench. Brenda Louise followed them. McClure had conquered Rosie, the toughest kid in school—just like that.

The choir started warming up. Mr. Gerald tapped the middle C key on the piano over and over again, and as they hummed, Brenda Louise remembered when Rosie had given her the name Metal Mouth.

It had been earlier that summer, on the play-field. Brenda Louise had seen a bunch of kids standing in a tight circle. She'd heard Rosie yelling the kind of words Rosie was famous for, the kind that gets parents mad. But the tone of her voice was different that day. She sounded scared.

Brenda Louise ran over and pushed through the kids. Rosie was lying on the ground. She was getting smeared by a big kid—a bully named Robert. He was punching her and calling her names. Rosie was shouting names at him, too, and since she was lying on the ground, it didn't seem wise for her to be calling him much of anything.

Everything Robert said he spat out like it was so much slime, all the while pounding Rosie. Brenda Louise looked at everybody in the circle.

Why didn't someone stop them? All the kids standing around were older and bigger, too. But nobody moved. Finally, she couldn't stand it. With her heart thumping, Brenda Louise started dancing around Robert and Rosie, yelling, "Let her go!"

She dashed in closer and the other kids moved back. She felt them recede like a wave on the beach. Robert hit Rosie again.

She couldn't let him do that! Brenda Louise leaped on Robert's back and pounded him as hard and fast as she could.

"Run, Rosie, run!" she yelled.

Robert swung. He swatted Brenda Louise like a fly. *Pow!* She saw red and green—blue—beautiful blues. A kaleidoscope. *Bam!* Brenda Louise clung to Robert's shirt so that she wouldn't fall down and tried to smile so that she wouldn't look scared.

The smile didn't fool anyone. But Rosie took her chance. She rolled, jumped up, and took off like lightning.

Backing away from Robert, Brenda Louise saw the kids watching her, their eyes big. There was a warm, salty taste in her mouth. She wiped the back of her hand across her chin. She scratched her hand, just running it over her mouth. She looked down. Her hand was smeared with blood. The wires on her braces had popped. She could feel them sticking out.

Robert lunged again. Brenda Louise turned and

ran, then crouched and raced through the tall grass along the hedges. The shadow by her side was Rosie. They finally reached Paradise Lane and collapsed on the grass in front of Brenda Louise's house.

Rosie looked at Brenda Louise, her eyes opened wide. Then she laughed and laughed, holding her sides and rolling in the grass.

"Metal Mouth," she said between gasps.

Brenda Louise got up slowly and limped away.

Rosie followed her. "You look so funny."

Brenda Louise turned and glared at Rosie, her mouth full of scratchy wires. Ungrateful Rosie. Brenda Louise suddenly sympathized with Robert. She wouldn't mind taking a swipe at Rosie herself.

"You aren't really hurt, are you?" Rosie asked.

Brenda Louise continued to walk, stiff-legged, to the house.

Rosie called out again. "Brenda Louise." She paused. "Thanks."

Brenda Louise kept walking, sweaty and tired, tears streaming down her face.

They'd tolerated each other ever since. Not many people could say that about Rosie.

Brenda Louise was suddenly aware of the choir room and the director tapping his baton. Her memories faded.

"Terrible—you sounded terrible." He glared at

the girls, sighed, and shrugged his shoulders. *"Again!"*

The choir started singing. Mr. Gerald slammed the keyboard cover down. Brenda Louise jumped. He looked straight up at McClure.

"Who are you?" he demanded.

Brenda Louise stood up. "Mr. Gerald, this is my friend McClure."

"It would be nice, Brenda Louise, if you'd introduced us earlier. *Never mind.*" Brenda Louise could tell that he minded a lot. "Well, McClure, what do you sing? Alto or soprano?" he asked impatiently.

"I don't know, sir. I've never sung in a choir before," said McClure.

Mr. Gerald moved his hands in the air. "Ah, she doesn't know! Try this." He handed her a sheet of music. Everyone was quiet and turned around to look.

"Mr. Gerald, let her sing with my group," Brenda Louise pleaded.

"It's okay, Brenda Louise," McClure said. She stood up. Mr. Gerald played a few notes on the piano, and McClure sang. Her voice was clear and sweet. Mr. Gerald smiled. He added chords to the melody as he played. When the music stopped, McClure sat down.

Wow! McClure could *really* sing.

Mr. Gerald was impressed, too. "I'm glad to

have you here, McClure," he said.

Brenda Louise gawked at him. He didn't say that to just anybody.

McClure and Rosie ended up walking together in the processional. In fact, they led the choir into the church. Rosie's voice was mellow and low. It harmonized with McClure's clear voice rising high above it. It was a natural assignment. Brenda Louise had never heard the choir sound so good. She should be happy. After all, she'd sneaked McClure into choir, and here McClure was leading it.

But Brenda Louise walked alone. Not only that, she walked at the very end of the line. Everybody had a partner but her.

It wasn't fair. She and McClure should be leading together, even though her own voice was nothing special. Actually, Kimberley always told her that she sang off-key. How could Kimberley know, anyway? Brenda Louise usually sang really softly, just in case Kimberley was right.

It wasn't good to watch, from the end of the line, how the congregation turned and smiled at Rosie and McClure. Not good at all to hear Mrs. Moody, the president of the Altar Guild, tell her husband, "At last they have some *real* singers."

The whole thing made Brenda Louise sick. She broke her rule about singing in choir. She sang loud. The incense curled around her and her voice rose. Inside, Brenda Louise felt sad. Outside, she smiled. She hoped her braces glittered in the light.

After church, Rosie and McClure waited for Brenda Louise in the choir room.

"You saved the day," said McClure.

Brenda Louise looked up at McClure as she unsnapped her choir robe.

"Yeah," said Rosie. "I didn't even know you could sing like that."

"Like what?" Brenda Louise asked. She felt her face getting red.

Rosie stood with her hands on her hips. "Stop playing dumb, Metal Mouth. You know. It was your voice that carried us up there. The organ music drowned all the rest of us out."

Brenda Louise stared at her. "You mean, I sounded okay? I wasn't off-key?"

Rosie cackled. "Is that what you thought?" She laughed again, and McClure grinned. Brenda Louise wished Rosie was quieter. The room was filling up with kids from choir.

"Brenda Louise, fine job, fine job," Mr. Gerald said as he rushed through the room.

Wow! Maybe they were right!

She saw Kimberley sail by and disappear around the corner. "Let's go," Brenda Louise told McClure. Rosie walked with them to the parking lot. It was turning into a beautiful, sunny day.

"It's a fine day for flying," said McClure. She swung her arms out and ran down the walkway.

Brenda Louise glared at her. Didn't McClure know flying wasn't something you tell just *anybody* about? It was special. Rosie'd make fun of them.

Brenda Louise tried to get McClure to meet her eyes so that she could warn her not to say any more. She did a little skip.

"What's wrong with you?" Rosie demanded.

"Nothing, nothing at all," Brenda Louise replied, and did a pirouette on the walkway. McClure never noticed. Finally, Brenda Louise hung back and walked regular, keeping in step.

"My Uncle Ben's coming out from New York today," McClure said. "He's getting in late this afternoon."

"You can still stay with us," Brenda Louise said as she kicked a pebble.

"No, I can't. I've got to get my stuff over to Hill House. But you can both come over!" McClure smiled at Brenda Louise.

"You've only been at our house for two days," Brenda Louise told her. She kicked another pebble, real hard. She didn't want McClure to go.

"You can both come over this afternoon. The housekeeper's there already." McClure started to walk fast. "Ask your parents, Rosie."

"My parents!" Rosie hooted. "They split three years ago. Everyone knows that. I live with Granny."

"Ask *her* then," said McClure matter-of-factly.

Rosie nodded. "I'll come after lunch. Are you sure I can get through the gate?"

"It's open now. It's only locked when no one's at home," said McClure.

Rosie left them at the path. She ran down to the lower road. "See ya!" she yelled.

"Come on, we'll miss our ride." Brenda Louise ran toward the parking lot.

Kimberley stood outside her father's car. "We've been waiting for over half an hour," she complained.

"Then you must have snuck out of church early," Brenda Louise said. She climbed into the backseat. The inside of the car reeked of her necklace. The smell filled her nostrils. She couldn't wait till Kimberley got a strong whiff.

"Lovely service today," Mr. Ryan said. "You have a nice, strong voice, Brenda Louise."

Brenda Louise smiled. If Kimberley didn't say she had sung off-key, then maybe she *had* sung okay. Kimberley would be the first one to point out whatever Brenda Louise had done wrong.

Kimberley glared at Brenda Louise. "I don't see what you're smiling about. You were too loud. No one could hear anyone else." She sniffed the air and made a face.

Brenda Louise looked at McClure. They tried not to laugh as the car sped along the road. Brenda Louise held the smelly necklace close to the back of Kimberley's seat. It was almost a shame they planned to bury it.

She looked out the window. Too bad McClure's uncle was coming, but McClure could still visit. She'd only be up the hill. They'd have lots of fun. And it *was* a good day for flying. Brenda Louise tried to forget that McClure had invited Rosie to Hill House, too.

No one's home," Brenda Louise told Mc-Clure. They'd run through the house, looking for Mom. "I was hoping she'd be here so she could give us a ride up the hill."

"It'll only take us five minutes to walk," Mc-Clure answered as she changed into her Hawaiian-print shorts and a pink T-shirt.

"I can't just leave. I need to tell my parents where we're going." As Brenda Louise talked, she looked in her drawer, trying to find a clean pair of shorts.

"Leave a note. But hurry. Rosie will be waiting," McClure said.

Brenda Louise didn't want to hurry. It wouldn't bother her if Rosie forgot to meet them. They didn't need Rosie.

"A note might get lost," she told McClure.

"We'll anchor it under the telephone." McClure looked at Brenda Louise. "We don't want Rosie to go home. This is going to be fun."

Brenda Louise didn't think McClure was right. Fun would have been just her and McClure flying. She should have said something to McClure before, about keeping flying secret. She held up some wrinkled blue shorts and put them on. They'd have to do.

"Here. You can write on this." McClure handed Brenda Louise an old envelope.

Brenda Louise wrote in big block letters: "Going to McClure's house. Love, B.L."

"It'll take us awhile to get ready. You pack, and I'll make lunch. And we should bury my necklace. Mom may be back by then."

"I don't need to pack. Most of my stuff is in the trunk at Hill House. I just have two suitcases down here, and they're all packed. I'll help you make sandwiches. We can eat on the way." McClure grabbed the necklace and ran to the back door. "I'll bury this. I'll be right back." The screen door slammed as she ran out.

Brenda Louise stood there, thinking. Climbing the hill would take a lot longer than five minutes. Rosie might give up and go home. That would be great. Not that she didn't *like* Rosie. It's just that Brenda Louise wanted McClure for herself. Rosie might spoil flying. She might spoil everything. Brenda Louise moved in slow motion to the kitchen. She really wanted a best friend, and McClure was almost it, like she'd wished. But not quite; not yet.

McClure bounded up the porch steps and burst into the kitchen. She rubbed her hands, dusting off the dirt. "I buried it. I put a stone there to mark it. We'll have to leave it out until school starts—to give the ants a chance."

"Thanks, McClure." Brenda Louise grinned, remembering Kimberley's reaction to the stink. She took a loaf of bread out of the cupboard. "We can make peanut butter sandwiches for our hike. It'll be hot out there. We'll need something to drink, too," she said.

"Okay, I'll go get my stuff."

A few minutes later, Brenda Louise heard a bumping noise on the stairs. "I'll help." She ran up the stairs and took one of the suitcases. "What's in here?" she asked as she tried to lift it. "It's heavy!"

"Important stuff. Shells. Foreign coins. Stuff like that."

"Neat! Can I see?"

McClure started bumping her other suitcase down the steps. "I'll show you when we get to my house. When there's more time."

There would be plenty of time now, Brenda Louise thought, if only Rosie wasn't going to meet them. She watched as Mr. Brown ran up and down the steps and in and out of the kitchen.

"Let's go," yelled McClure from the front door. She had a suitcase in one hand and one of the peanut butter sandwiches in the other.

"I'm coming." Brenda Louise had dawdled all she could. She shoved McClure's other suitcase with her foot as she closed the front door, holding her peanut butter sandwich with her teeth.

The road before them went straight up the hill. They trudged up slowly. Halfway there, panting, they sat down, using the suitcases as chairs.

"It's farther than I thought," McClure said. She wiped her forehead. "Hotter, too." She held the bottom of her T-shirt out. "My shirt's sticking to me."

"We forgot to bring something to drink," Brenda Louise said, trying to chew her sandwich. The peanut butter stuck to the roof of her mouth and made it hard to talk.

McClure stood up and started walking again. "We're almost there. I can see the gate at the top of the hill."

Trudging along behind her, Brenda Louise could see the big trees and lots of lawn. "It looks cool," she said as they walked toward the shade. She mopped her forehead with the bottom of her shirt. Hill House hid among the big trees, way back from the road, looking the same as ever. It was like McClure had never left at all.

Mr. Brown walked beside them, his tongue hanging out, panting.

"I wonder where Rosie is," McClure said.

Brenda Louise looked down at her feet, not wanting to meet McClure's eyes. "Maybe she got tired of waiting for us."

"Do you think so?" McClure asked. "Gosh, I hope not. She'd be just perfect as a Flying Chicken."

"She would?" Brenda Louise asked.

"Well, sure," said McClure. "First off, she's *your* friend. And she's tough. You've gotta have guts to fly."

"That's true." Brenda Louise took a deep breath. Maybe Rosie wouldn't be so bad after all. She *was* sort of a friend—as much as Rosie could be a friend. Brenda Louise could teach Rosie like she'd taught McClure. She could have two best friends.

Maybe.

But what if McClure and Rosie became really good friends together, just the two of them? Her heart sank at the thought.

And, with that, who should walk up the drive, right behind them, but Rosie herself.

Brenda Louise felt a little foolish. She wasn't usually so suspicious. But if she made a big deal about Rosie and tried to exclude her, the worse *she* would look.

"Rosie," she called, reckless. "How would you like to join a secret club?"

"Who belongs?" Rosie asked, chewing on a big wad of bubble gum.

"Me, McClure, and Mr. Brown."

"Who's Mr. Brown?" Rosie stood looking at them. Then she looked down at Mr. Brown lying in the grass, panting. "The dog?"

"We'll all be officers. I'm president, McClure's vice president, and you'll be treasurer. We don't have dues or anything; not yet, anyway."

"Doesn't this club have any regular members? Are we all officers?"

"We're officers *and* members." Brenda Louise gave Rosie a cold stare. Rosie didn't seem to realize how close she was to being a nonmember.

"That's the funniest thing I ever heard," Rosie said.

She didn't show any respect at all, but then,

Rosie wouldn't. It *was* sort of funny, though, and Brenda Louise smiled.

"Let's go flying right now," said McClure.

"Flying? You don't know anyone who owns a plane"—Rosie snapped her gum—"do you?"

McClure and Brenda Louise looked at each other and grinned.

"We'll show you the *kind* of flying we mean." Brenda Louise tugged at one of the suitcases. "First, help us get these suitcases over to the house."

Rosie grabbed a suitcase. "This ought to be interesting," she said.

McClure pointed to the field below them. "There's a place down there that'll be great for flying."

Rosie stopped dragging the suitcase and looked at the field. "You want us to fly down there? I thought just Brenda Louise was off her rocker, but you're both crazy."

It was going to be okay. Brenda Louise knew it. But then she remembered something. She looked at the three of them, wearing short-sleeved shirts, shorts, and sandals. "We could get poison ivy in that field, and ticks, too. We'll need jeans and long socks. I just wish it wasn't so hot." Ticks were the biggest problem. After all, they could see poison ivy. It wasn't so easy to see a tiny tick.

"We can get stuff from my trunk. I've got lots of jeans and socks," McClure said.

"It would help if you carried clothes in your suitcases," Brenda Louise muttered.

"The stuff I've got in here is better than clothes. I'll show you later, like I promised." McClure wiped her forehead as she talked.

Finally, they reached the house. Rosie flopped down on the steps. McClure ran up to the door. She looked around the driveway. "The housekeeper isn't here. The car's gone." She frowned. "She must be at the store."

"How are we going to get inside?" Brenda Louise sat down on one of the suitcases.

"I've got a key," McClure said, pulling at the chain around her neck. "Here we go!" She opened the door. They left the suitcases in the kitchen. "Come on," she yelled as she bounded up the stairs. Brenda Louise and Rosie ran up behind her.

McClure opened a big black trunk in the middle of her room. Clothes popped out of the top.

"Wow," said Rosie. She took the wad of bubble gum out of her mouth and wrapped it in two gum wrappers. "Look at all this stuff." She lifted a yellow sweater up from the pile of clothes.

"How'd you ever keep the top on?" Brenda Louise asked. It didn't seem possible that all those things had ever fit inside.

"My dad had to stand on top so we could close it." McClure stood in the middle of the big pile of clothes. "Just look at this!" She tugged at some ski underwear. "This will be perfect." She sat down and pulled on the ski underwear.

Rosie rummaged through the pile of clothes and pulled out a pair of white ballet tights.

"Okay if I use these?" she asked. "And these ski socks?"

McClure nodded. "Sure. The tights may be torn. I used them for ballet class." She yanked her Hawaiian-print shorts up over her ski underwear. "Try my cowgirl boots. They're the only things I have that'll fit over those socks."

"There isn't anything left for me," Brenda Louise said. She kicked the pile of clothes with her foot. Whatever made her think they could all be friends? "It's too hot to wear this stuff, anyway."

"I've got just the thing," said McClure. She tossed a tennis racket onto the bed and poked around in the pile of clothes, pulling out a pair of blue pajama bottoms. "Aren't these the greatest?"

"They're okay, I guess."

Actually they were better than okay—the pajama bottoms were deep sky blue, a perfect flying color. Brenda Louise pulled them on and stuffed the bottoms into another pair of ski socks. She eyed the tennis racket McClure had tossed onto the bed. She'd almost forgotten about tennis lessons. She turned away. No reason to spoil things by thinking about tennis.

"We're going to boil, wearing all this stuff in this heat," Rosie said.

"We're not only going to boil," Brenda Louise told her, "we're going to sizzle and fry."

McClure made a face. "You're right. But we won't get ticks—and we look fabulous. Come on! Let's stand in front of the mirror," she said.

"Who gets to wear McClure's jacket?" Rosie asked. She smoothed the soft leather with her hands.

McClure and Brenda Louise looked at each other. Brenda Louise shrugged. "I guess you can," she said. "It'll be way too hot."

"The heat won't stop me." Rosie slipped the jacket on and stood in front of the mirror. "How do I look?"

The jacket hung down over her shorts. Her legs were covered with McClure's white ballet tights. Every time Rosie took a step, she clumped because the boots were too big. But there was no getting around it: If you squinted your eyes, Rosie looked like a real aviator.

"You look classic," said McClure. "Absolutely classic."

Brenda Louise looked at their reflection in the mirror. "We look grand," she announced.

"One more thing," McClure said. "We need to wear our sunglasses. All true fliers wear sunglasses, to cut down on the glare."

"Of course," said Brenda Louise, putting her glasses on. *"Now* we are ready!"

"You two are crazy," said Rosie as she clumped along after them. But she put on a pair of sunglasses, too.

They marched out of McClure's bedroom, down the stairs, and out the back door. Mr. Brown pranced beside them.

"The second meeting of the Flying Chickens is about to begin!" announced McClure.

Follow the leader," yelled McClure as she stretched her arms out like the wings on a plane. She ran down the field, with Brenda Louise and Rosie running behind her. They stopped at the bottom of the field, just before the fence.

McClure shoved her sunglasses on top of her head and studied the split-rail fence. "I can't remember exactly where I thought the best place would be—everything looks different from the last time I was down here."

"You've been away a long time," Brenda Louise reminded her. "Things change."

Rosie and Mr. Brown flopped on the grass. Rosie pulled the riding boots off her feet and wiggled her toes. She took the World War II genuine leather aviator jacket off and laid it next to Mr. Brown.

"I get the jacket next," Brenda Louise said.

Rosie turned toward Brenda Louise, scrunching her eyes into two tiny slits. "You have a problem with me wearing this here jacket?" she asked.

"No, not at all." Brenda Louise gave her "guaranteed-to-shrivel-their-insides-look" back to Rosie.

Rosie stood up. She didn't seem bothered by the evil eye. In fact, she didn't seem to notice it at all.

"This is *it*. This is *the* place. Come on!" yelled McClure. She strode over to another section of the fence and clambered up the rails. On the very top, she stood and swayed back and forth.

"How can you tell this is the place? It looks the same as the fence over there." Brenda Louise pointed to the left.

"It has a level landing ground. It'll be perfect." McClure grinned down at her.

Rosie stood real stiff as she watched McClure sway. "It looks high," she said.

"Aw, nothing to it," Brenda Louise said as she scrambled up after McClure. It wasn't easy with all the stuff she had on. She'd never admit it, but Rosie was right. It was high. It scared Brenda

Louise to death. "We'll show you how flying is done," she told Rosie.

Brenda Louise perched next to McClure, her pajama bottoms rippling in the breeze. They could see the whole meadow below. But when Brenda Louise looked straight down, goose bumps ran over her like a shiver. A shiver in the heat. Rosie looked up at them, her eyes big. Brenda Louise knew the fence wasn't as high as the end of the garage, but the fence wasn't solid like the garage. It was open and scary. Like stairs without backs. It *seemed* higher. And it stuck straight up from the ground.

"Are you sure this is where beginners should start?" Rosie asked.

That's all Brenda Louise needed to hear. She stood straight then, balancing the wind.

"We'll help you," she told Rosie.

"It's mostly mental, Rosie," McClure explained. "You've got to want to fly, *wish* very hard, and give yourself a chance to do it."

"Let's go," Brenda Louise yelled, grabbing McClure's hand. Together they leaped off the top of the fence. Rosie shrieked and Mr. Brown barked, the wind whistled, and Brenda Louise was flying. Then the ground came up so fast, suddenly, and McClure and Brenda Louise tumbled out of the sky. They landed on either side of Rosie.

"Why, you're only jumping," Rosie complained in disgust.

"That's what it looks like," Brenda Louise admitted. "But once you try it, you'll see."

McClure put an arm around Rosie's shoulders. "That's what makes it so great. Most people don't know."

Rosie didn't look convinced; her lower lip stuck out. But McClure had already climbed the fence again. She stood outlined against the sky, her ski underwear puckered at the knees.

Rosie looked tiny next to the fence. She pulled the cowgirl boots back on over her socks, slipped McClure's World War II jacket on, and climbed up. Brenda Louise followed.

Rosie slowly drew herself up, like a ballet dancer, cautiously balancing between McClure and Brenda Louise.

"You want to go solo, or with us?" McClure asked.

"It's too high." Rosie lurched back and forth. They swayed. "Uh-oh." Her face paled.

"Remember to close your eyes," McClure told her.

"Close my eyes! You're both crazy," Rosie retorted.

"Are you chicken?" Brenda Louise asked.

"Yup," answered Rosie, and then the three of

them giggled. Back and forth they went, their arms out of balance.

"We are the Flying Chickens!" yelled McClure.

"We go *together*," Rosie said. She grabbed them both by the hand.

"Take off!" McClure shouted.

Brenda Louise heard Mr. Brown yapping below. She heard herself scream, heard Rosie and McClure scream, too. *It was wonderful.*

They landed with a thud and stared at each other. Rosie grinned. "That's fun." She picked herself up and brushed off the white tights. "Let's do it again."

"I thought you'd like it," Brenda Louise said.

They ran to the fence for the next flight. This time they looked out over the field and across at the far ridge. They were part of the sky, part of the wind. They swayed on top of the wobbly fence. Rosie and McClure grabbed Brenda Louise by the hands. The Flying Chickens flew into the sun.

As Brenda Louise waited for her tennis lesson, she looked out at the ocean and wished she were swimming. Instead, she stood baking on the tennis court, the heat melting the bottoms of her sneakers. She was probably already stuck to the ground.

"Oh-kay," Nicky announced. Brenda Louise was in his last tennis class of the morning. He wiped the sweat off his forehead with a towel.

"Brenda Louise, your racket, please." Nicky held his hand out.

Brenda Louise dragged Mom's old racket from

behind her back. No one else had anything that looked like it. Kimberley had a brand-new racket. Brenda Louise sighed. Nicky smoothed the wood and ran his fingers over the strings. At one end, there were a few unraveled strands.

"You'll need new strings, but it's a grand old racket. Watch." He made a graceful arc with Mom's racket. Then he bounced a ball and swung again in a lazy, easy motion. There was a dull thud when the two connected. The ball rolled away. He picked up another racket, bounced another ball, and made the same easy arc. The racket pinged. This time the ball sailed over the net.

"Use my racket today. We'll restring this one."

"Ask him what they use," Kimberley said. She pushed her sunglasses back on her nose.

"Ask him yourself." Brenda Louise held Nicky's racket. It was light and beautiful.

"Catgut—that's what they use," Kimberley said.

"Aw, come on—give me a break."

"It's true," Nicky said.

"You mean they kill cats so people can play tennis?" Brenda Louise held Nicky's racket by the handle now, far away from the strings. She didn't really like cats, but she didn't want them to become tennis strings. "That's gross, Nicky."

"If you want to get specific, they don't use cats at all. They use the dried intestines of horses and sheep," Nicky said.

"Horses?" Brenda Louise loved horses. It was another good reason not to learn this dumb game.

Nicky stood there with his hands on his hips and grinned at her. "Don't worry. We'll use synthetics, if you want. But some people still consider gut to be the best."

"That's okay. No guts." Brenda Louise swung his racket in the air, pretending she was hitting the ball.

Nicky watched her carefully. "Just what I thought. You hold the racket like a natural."

Amazed, Brenda Louise looked down at her hand and back at him. "What?"

"Perfect forehand position." He turned to the class. "Today you practice forehand on the backboard. Tomorrow you practice. Every day you practice." He smiled and handed them a bucket of balls. Off they went.

Everybody had their own space. All you could hear was *slam, bam, slam* as the balls hit the backboard. Only, not everybody hit the backboard. In fact, that first day, most everybody hit the balls so hard, they sailed right over the backboard and plunked down in the parking lot.

Kimberley stood next to Brenda Louise. "All we do is chase tennis balls," she complained.

"Tennis is like that when you start." Nicky had walked up behind them. "It'll get better."

Brenda Louise had her doubts.

"I give up," Billy Roscoe yelled. He threw his racket on the ground. "This game stinks." He stomped off the court.

He was right. Tennis wasn't any fun—it was hard work. But Brenda Louise was stuck there. She kept watching as kids sneaked away. They went off the court to chase balls and never came back. She wanted to tell Mom that everyone had quit the class. That was a good idea! Then she could visit with McClure.

But when Brenda Louise talked to Mom, Mom didn't understand at all. "This is something we want you to do, Brenda Louise. You have to give it a chance."

"I gave it a chance."

"Nicky says you are doing wonderfully."

"Really?" Brenda Louise was pleased. "See, Mom, I tried. But I need a break now."

But Mom didn't give in.

Brenda Louise was one of the few left in class. It made her mad, sweltering in the sun, hitting balls against the old board. *Slam, bam, slam.* Endless hitting and missing.

But by the end of the week, she could hit the ball exactly where she wanted to. She scooped balls up off the court with a flip of her racket. Yet she still steamed.

"When is Nicky going to let you play a game?" Rosie leaned into the wire fence as she watched

Brenda Louise practice. The day before, she'd pelted Brenda Louise with tennis balls from the parking lot. Rosie hung around the courts. She knew everything about all the top players. Rosie couldn't afford tennis lessons, but then, she didn't need them. She was really good.

"I'm not sure he'll ever let us," answered Brenda Louise. "We're pretty bad."

Brenda Louise looked at the beach and longed to be in the cool water. She wondered what McClure was doing up at Hill House. They still got to see each other, but not often enough. Tennis took too much time. But the next day, something wonderful happened: It started to rain.

It rained hard for two days. Brenda Louise stared out the window. She was so glad about not playing tennis, she almost didn't realize that rain grounded the Flying Chickens, too.

But they wouldn't be grounded if they flew *indoors*! She jumped up and walked around the living room. It just might work. They could fly there! Why, she'd shove the furniture against the wall and make a big space for flying.

When Mom had banned her from flying in the living room, she had really been quite specific: No more leaping off the couch or jumping from the stairs. They were flying now in a much more advanced way—they wouldn't get near the stairs, and they'd move the couch out of the way altogether. And since Mom was at the dentist, well, she didn't need to know. Tom wouldn't have to know, either.

Brenda Louise called Rosie.

"You're crazy. How can we fly inside?" Rosie asked.

"Get over here and see," Brenda Louise answered.

It *would* work. She imagined them leaping across the room, flying to the ceiling. She'd have McClure demonstrate the ballet way. Dancers flew inside all the time. Rosie would have to eat her words.

She dialed McClure's number and told her about flying. "And McClure, bring some Music to Fly By." Brenda Louise wanted everything to be right. "Like some Tchaikovsky Music to Fly By."

Brenda Louise moved furniture, clearing an open space. Rosie and McClure showed up before she was finished. Together they moved the couch against the wall and rolled up the rug.

And now, with the music thundering through the room, even Rosie seemed impressed. Just like a ballet dancer, McClure leaped across the room, flying higher and higher. Brenda Louise held her breath. McClure drifted to the floor. She was good, really good.

"I want to go next," Rosie said.

"It's my turn," Brenda Louise said.

But when she and Rosie tried to imitate Mc-Clure, they collided in the air. Brenda Louise limped, rubbing first her leg, then her shoulder.

"That sure didn't work out," Brenda Louise said.

"I told you it wouldn't." Rosie glared at her.

Tom yelled at them from the stairs. "Turn the music down! I can't hear the phone!"

"You should talk," Brenda Louise yelled back. "You always have music loud."

"Yeah, but I don't shake the whole house at the same time. You sound like flying elephants."

Brenda Louise turned the music off. Flying indoors had seemed like such a good idea. Suddenly it hit her. "I've got an idea," she said, "for quiet flying."

She walked over to the French windows. They opened out like folding doors, and they went all the way to the floor. "If we flew from somewhere, like this windowsill, into the garden, we wouldn't make much noise. And it isn't like a real garden, one that we could hurt. Nothing's growing there."

"No. But we'd get wet," Rosie said.

McClure opened the tall windows. "It isn't raining as hard."

"It looks muddy." Rosie leaned out the window. "It's too far down."

"I think it's a perfect place for the Flying Chickens," Brenda Louise announced. She didn't feel sore anymore. "Come on, Rosie, it'll be easy. The window isn't all that high."

"I'm putting my boots on for this flight," McClure said.

"So am I," Rosie said.

"Okay, I will, too." Brenda Louise ran to the hall closet and looked for her boots.

"Hurry up!"

Brenda Louise turned, her boots in her hand. There, filling the window ledge, stood McClure and Rosie, giggling.

"Hey, wait for me!" She pulled her boots on, hopping across the room.

"There isn't room for three of us," Rosie said.

"We'll fit." Brenda Louise held her breath in, trying to make herself as skinny as possible.

"Wait till we go!" McClure and Rosie yelled. They hurtled through the rain. Brenda Louise balanced on the ledge, then she jumped, too. Brenda Louise floated over the garden. It was a surprise to find so much mud when she landed bottom side down. Instant cold seeped around her shorts, her legs, and her hands.

"I'm stuck," McClure yelled. She'd landed feet first—her boots sunk deep.

"Me, too," Rosie said.

"Don't complain. At least you landed right side up," Brenda Louise said.

Rosie lurched forward as she tried to walk. Her right foot shot out of her boot and sank. She leaned forward, trying to balance. "Uh-oh!" Her left foot slipped out of the left boot. "Oh, *no!*" Rosie stood, trapped in thick goo. Behind Rosie were her boots, stuck where she'd landed.

McClure twisted around, laughing. "My boots are caught, too." When she scratched her chin, her hand left a muddy streak.

Brenda Louise crawled out of the garden, keeping her boots on. Mud squished through her fingers. When she reached the lawn, she stood up. She pulled mud out of her pockets. "Yuck! I'll get the hose and wash us off."

Rosie and McClure followed her, pulling their feet out of the mud. *Squish. Squash. Squish.*

"That was a neat flight," McClure said as she lurched through the mud. "The landing was our most unusual yet."

"It was better than the flying inside," Rosie said.

Brenda Louise pulled the hose over and sprayed McClure and Rosie.

"The water is *cold!*" McClure yelled.

"It's freezing," Rosie said, her teeth chattering together. "Here, I'll do you." She grabbed the hose from Brenda Louise and sprayed her.

Brenda Louise danced around in the water, shivering. "Let's get inside. We can get some towels and dry off."

"Brenda Louise!" Tom leaned out his bedroom window. "Mom just drove in the back way."

Brenda Louise felt her heart stop. Mom!

"Tom, fix the living room. *Please.*"

Tom grinned. He leaned on his elbows, as if he had plenty of time. "You'll owe me."

"Please!"

"You'll owe me plenty."

Scared, Brenda Louise turned and looked at Rosie and McClure. She shook her head. When she turned back, Tom had disappeared from the window.

Rosie shut the water off. "Maybe we better leave."

"We can get our boots later," McClure said.

"My ride should be coming soon. I'll wait out by the road." Rosie ran toward the side of the house. She stopped at the corner and made a thumbs-up.

McClure ran after Rosie. "Call me later," she yelled.

Brenda Louise waved as McClure ran. It was better that Mom didn't find them there. It was good that she parked in back. Brenda Louise took a last look at the garden. She saw the tops of Rosie's and McClure's boots growing in the mud.

Brenda Louise waited until she heard the back door slam. Taking a deep breath, she sloshed through the wet grass and walked up the front steps.

"Hi, Mom. I got a little wet." She stood at the front door, water dripping off her clothes.

"Brenda Louise, what in the world have you done?" Mom's voice went up an octave higher than usual. "You're soaked."

Mom grabbed some towels from the bathroom and wrapped them around Brenda Louise. "Look at the mud! You better take everything off." She looked at Brenda Louise from head to toe. "I've never seen you so dirty. What were you doing?"

Tom walked into the hallway. "Just what *were* you doing, Brenda Louise?" He smirked at her.

"Oh, Mom," Brenda Louise said, "it wasn't anything bad." She peeked into the living room. The furniture was back in place. Whew. She was going to owe Tom for this one.

"I've been inside all day," Tom said.

"Then you must have seen what was going on!"

Tom was suddenly quiet. Mom turned to Brenda Louise.

"You are going into the shower, right now. You also have some explaining to do." Mom stood there, hands on hips.

Brenda Louise ran into the bathroom and turned the water on.

What if Mom happened to look out the window and see the boots growing in the garden?

Brenda Louise dropped her muddy clothes on the floor and got into the shower. The shower made her forget Mom was mad. It made her feel good. When the room was steamy, she finally got out. In her room, she pulled on clean clothes. Then she ran downstairs.

"Brenda Louise." Mom leaned across the counter. "When you finish in here, I want you to clean every muddy footprint on the floor."

"Sure, Mom." Brenda Louise didn't mind. She was so grateful that Mom didn't know about the living room, she would have cleaned the whole house. "Mom, I'm sorry."

"What were you doing in the mud?" Suddenly, Mom didn't look so angry. "Never mind; I think I know. You were flying."

Brenda Louise nodded. She hopped between the chairs as she set the table. The rain stopped just before supper. She felt clean and fresh, just like it smelled outside after the rain. She danced around the kitchen, helping.

"Mom, remember when you said someday McClure and I'd be friends again? Well, you were right."

She thought of Rosie. She was a friend, too, sort of.

"We've got a secret club, Mom. Even Rosie's in it. And Mr. Brown. I'm going to learn French. Lots of it. I'm so happy now that McClure's here." She just blurted it out. Mom was quiet. But Brenda Louise couldn't stop talking.

"Even school's going to be great." She smiled just to think of it.

"Brenda Louise, McClure's uncle called us today." Mom stood by the stove.

"Why?" Brenda Louise asked. Mom's voice sounded different.

"McClure can't stay," Mom said.

"Can't stay? What do you mean? She just got here."

"Her parents want her to go to school in Europe."

Brenda Louise felt a lump growing in her throat. "She can't go. We just started being friends again. It isn't fair." She leaned against the kitchen chair. She thought of Mr. Brown. She'd lose him, too. Her eyes felt wet. Tears splashed down her face. She sniffled.

"Everything was going great." Brenda Louise gulped in air and sniffled again.

"She won't be going until the end of summer."

"The end of summer? That's practically here!" Brenda Louise wiped her eyes. "Why can't she stay? It isn't fair."

"I'm sorry, Brenda Louise." Mom moved the pan off the stove. "She doesn't get to stay anywhere very long."

Brenda Louise stared out the window. McClure *had* to stay. They would have to think of something. After all, now the three of them knew how to fly. Anything else should be easy!

"Nicky called today, too," Mom said. "He said the courts are wet, but classes will start up again tomorrow. The rain seems to have stopped."

Brenda Louise scowled. He wouldn't even wait till the courts dried.

The next morning, everything still looked drippy. "It's too wet, Mom," Brenda Louise said as she looked out the window. "They'll have to cancel tennis."

But Mom shook her head. "It'll be fine."

It wasn't fine at all. The tennis courts looked like lakes. Not lakes, exactly, but the puddles *were* big. It also wasn't any fun pushing the heavy broom around, sweeping the water off. When she started hitting against the backboard, the balls splashed on the spots she'd missed. And as the sun climbed in the sky, the courts steamed. Brenda Louise kept thinking about McClure.

"Backhand today. It can be difficult." Nicky stood in the middle of the steam and demonstrated.

His voice intruded on her thoughts. Backhand! Difficult wasn't the right word. Backhand was impossible. All the expertise Brenda Louise had built practicing the forehand didn't seem to matter. She was back at the beginning.

By the time the courts were completely dry, it was time to go. The paved area by the backboard was empty. It reminded her of Paradise Lane when McClure wasn't there.

13

he Flying Chickens held an emergency
meeting the next afternoon in the apple
tree behind the garage. McClure scooted up to the
highest branches. Rosie hung by her knees from a
low branch, and Brenda Louise lay across two
branches in the center of the tree.

It wasn't easy, thinking of a plan so McClure
could stay on Paradise Lane.

"We could hide you," Rosie said to McClure.
"Make you disappear."

McClure shook her head. "They'd find me.
Maybe I could have a disease no one has ever heard

of . . . one we invent. Then I'd have to stay at Hill House, and you guys could visit. . . ."

Brenda Louise frowned. "No. They would just get a doctor, and that would be the end of that."

"Okay, what *will* work?" Rosie asked.

Brenda Louise sighed. Then it hit her. "I've got an idea!" she said.

Rosie arched her eyebrows and smirked at McClure. She blew a big bubble with her gum, as if she thought that Brenda Louise's idea was stupid before she'd even heard it.

Brenda Louise glared at her. Rosie swung back and forth, hanging by her knees, the big pink bubble hiding her face.

"Advertising. We need to advertise and convince your parents to let you stay. You'll need to write them," Brenda Louise said.

"I never write. They move all the time," McClure said.

"We'll bombard them. We'll send stuff about Paradise Lane. About school," Brenda Louise said, smiling.

"It won't work, Metal Mouth." Rosie's face was red from hanging upside down for so long.

"It's better than not trying at all, Rosie." Brenda Louise grabbed a branch and dropped down to the ground. "When your parents get here, McClure, I'll give a talk to persuade them."

"It's worth a try. I'll write today," McClure said.

"Well, maybe it'll work," said Rosie. "I vote we meet at the beach snack bar tomorrow. I have to help Granny down there, anyway."

"I second Rosie," Brenda Louise said. "I have my tennis lesson. I'll be there, too." Her voice dropped when she talked about tennis.

McClure pulled the heels of her purple socks up out of her running shoes. The World War II genuine leather aviator jacket hid her shorts. She grabbed the highest hanging branch and dangled in the air. "I know a great place for flying," she said.

"Where?" Brenda Louise and Rosie asked at once.

"You'll have to wait till we get to the beach." McClure's low laugh sounded mysterious.

14

The Flying Chickens had to postpone their meeting at the beach. McClure visited her Aunt Julia and stayed an extra week. By the time they finally met, it was dead low tide, the lowest the tide could be. The beach was deserted.

Brenda Louise had already put in a good hour on the tennis court, placing long shots over the net to Kimberley. It was one of her better lessons. She liked making Kimberley run all over the court. After the lesson, Brenda Louise looked through the wire fence, mopping her face with a towel. She could see McClure and Rosie waiting on the beach near the snack bar. The air smelled of salt and the mud of the tide flats. Beyond the bathhouses, the water out in the channel looked like a shiny ribbon.

Brenda Louise left her racket with Nicky. She kicked off her sneakers and stuffed her socks inside. She tied the laces together and hung the sneakers around her neck. Then she ran through the sand to the snack bar where Rosie's grandmother worked, the sneakers banging against her. Brenda Louise ran up just as Rosie's granny peered across the counter.

"What's that miserable creature doing here?" She pointed a bony finger at Mr. Brown. "Don't you know the rules? No dogs on the beach. No exceptions."

Mr. Brown put his tail between his legs. He might not know English, but he could tell from her tone that he wasn't welcome.

"This dog is different," Rosie said. "He's from France. He doesn't know American rules."

Granny stood there, her hands on her hips. "Don't try to fool me!"

"It's true. You have to speak French to him."

"Well, that leaves you out," said Granny.

Rosie whistled at Mr. Brown. *"Bonjour, Monsieur* Brown," she said. *"Voici* Granny."

Brenda Louise was surprised. Rosie? Speaking French? Granny looked surprised, too. Mr. Brown padded across the boardwalk to Granny and lay down by the snack bar.

"I don't believe it," Granny said.

But just the same, Granny's face didn't look so grumpy. She nodded at them. "Well, Rosie, you can run off now—no one's around here, anyway. But mind you, when the tide comes in, I expect you *here*."

McClure slipped off the World War II genuine leather aviator jacket and laid in on the counter. "Would you watch this for us?" she asked. She wore big sunglasses shoved up on the top of her head. She grinned and looked at Granny. Granny reached out and smoothed the leather jacket.

"This is the real thing, isn't it? You don't want to leave it here. It'll smell like a snack bar," Granny said.

McClure shrugged. "That's okay. I'd be honored if you'd watch it."

McClure and her good manners! Granny's face crinkled up, and Brenda Louise realized that Granny was smiling. It was a first.

"I'll leave my sneakers in the corner," Brenda Louise said, "if that's okay." She didn't wait for Granny to say no. Instead, she darted after McClure and Rosie, running to the water, lickety-split.

"Hurry," Rosie said, "before she changes her mind about letting me go."

Mr. Brown bounded after them. The water was so calm that there were only tiny ripples running up onto the sand. McClure splashed as she ran in the shallow water. She held her arms out and so did Brenda Louise. Brenda Louise felt like she was running into the sky, flying across the sand. All she could hear was the water splashing as they ran. The beach swallowed up sounds, muffling them.

"The horseshoe crabs are here," she yelled, and ran alongside McClure. There were at least ten big crabs by the rocks of the breakwater. That's when she remembered the crab she'd saved for McClure, still in the shoe box in the garage.

"I was going to send you one," she gasped, her voice coming out unevenly as she ran. "It's all wrapped up. I forgot to give it to you."

"Remember when you get home," McClure yelled back.

McClure had a way of making people feel okay. Brenda Louise leaped into the air, her feet landing in the black, squishy low-tide sand. The sand squirted through her toes. It was a *wonderful* day.

"Wait for me," Rosie called out. She was running zigzag in and out of the water, racing the ripples.

Brenda Louise swooped down and grabbed a big horseshoe crab by its tail. As she lifted it up, the crab wriggled its legs. She lunged toward McClure and giggled as McClure danced sideways. Mr.

Brown sniffed the crab, backing away, growling.

Bending down, McClure looked at the crabs by her feet. "Do you think they can see?" She pointed to the bumps on the shell.

Brenda Louise shrugged. "They've got nine eyes, but I don't think it helps—having so many."

"They're prehistoric." Rosie panted as she reached them, her words rushed. "It's true. I learned it in science class."

Brenda Louise crouched next to McClure, down with the crabs. "They were here before dinosaurs. They're the *oldest* creatures on earth." She thought of the horseshoe crab she'd found for McClure—it was the most special gift anyone could get.

They were quiet then. They watched as the water lapped the beach, and the crabs crawled away, leaving trails in the sand with their tails.

"McClure, the one I got you is an empty shell—a baby one. I found it by the tide line," Brenda Louise said.

"You're giving her a dead horseshoe crab? Phew. I bet it's full of sand, and it'll make a mess all over everywhere." Rosie shook her head in disbelief.

Brenda Louise glared. "It's a wonderful gift. She can shake the sand out." She wanted to shake Rosie.

As they waded, they looked out toward the deep water.

"See the float?" Brenda Louise asked. "We could walk all the way out to it."

"That's the place," McClure said. "When the tide comes in, we can go flying off the diving board out there."

Brenda Louise studied the float. It was close to shore now—real easy to reach at low tide. At high tide, it'd be deep, over their heads. And the tide was coming in. She might be worn out, swimming that far. But McClure was right: It would be a perfect place for flying.

Rosie grinned. "It looks like a super place for the Flying Chickens. I could use a *soft* landing."

Brenda Louise nodded. She didn't want to be the only one who protested.

It was high tide.

"Our bathhouse locker is near here—you can both change with me," Brenda Louise said. They stood on the boardwalk looking down on the sand and water. Now there were people lying on beach towels, sitting under beach umbrellas. Children ran in and out of the water. The sky and the water swallowed up the noise. The beach was smaller with the high-water line.

"My bathing suit's back at the snack bar. Granny'll never let me go now. She said I had to be back at high tide." Rosie looked at the snack bar and frowned.

"I've got two bathing suits in our locker," Brenda Louise said. She grinned. "You can borrow one."

"I know I should check with Granny," Rosie said.

"Here's our bathhouse," Brenda Louise said, stopping at number thirty-nine. She felt in her pockets. "Only I forgot the key."

Rosie put her hands on her hips. "Great."

"No problem." Brenda Louise looked up and down the boardwalk. Nobody was looking. She backed up to the bathhouse door and hit it real fast with her backside. The door popped open.

McClure ran inside. "Isn't there a light in here?"

"You have to hook the door open," Brenda Louise answered. "That's the only way you can see."

"Yeah," said Rosie, "and be sure to check the floor."

"Why?" McClure asked.

"To see what's down there. To see if anybody's under the deck, looking up," Brenda Louise said.

The three of them knelt on the boardwalk and peered down.

"It's safe," Brenda Louise said. "Here's the suit you can borrow." She handed Rosie a bathing suit.

"What are you going to wear?" Rosie asked her.

Brenda Louise groped around the wall with her

hands. "This," she said, pulling last summer's suit off the hook. It smelled musty. When she held it up, sand fell out of the folds. But it seemed okay, just wrinkled and faded.

"Did you leave it here all year? Gross." Rosie shook her head.

Brenda Louise glared at her. "What's so gross? It's just sand."

"Does that old thing still fit you?" Rosie hooted. "Even if it doesn't fit, it's not like you've got to worry. You don't have anything to show."

Brenda Louise pulled her suit on. "A lot you know." Rosie thought she was so smart. Well, she didn't have anything more than Brenda Louise.

Brenda Louise unhooked the door. The light outside seemed blinding after the darkness. Her eyes focused on Rosie in her borrowed suit. Rosie looked great. Brenda Louise had never noticed before, but Rosie was pretty.

She looked down at her suit. The elastic didn't stretch anymore. She snuck a look at McClure. McClure's suit was blue. It was beautiful and shiny. And McClure looked tan and golden. Brenda Louise wished she had a French bathing suit to wear.

The three of them trooped out to the beach, stomping on the boardwalk. Just ahead, water glittered in the sun and the sand shimmered. Brenda Louise looked down toward the snack bar.

She couldn't tell if there was a line of people. The glare of sun made it hard to see.

"Come on," Rosie yelled as they leaped off the boardwalk.

"Last one in is a rotten egg," McClure shouted.

Brenda Louise hated to get her stomach wet. She took a deep breath and dived. The shock of the water made her shiver. Her teeth chattered. When she rubbed her arms, they were covered with goose bumps. She tried to swim a straight line out to the float.

McClure was way ahead. McClure swam perfectly. Not like her and Rosie.

Brenda Louise kept churning along. Every once in a while, she surfaced, took some big breaths, and bobbed up and down in the water. Then, finally, she bumped into the thick rope that kept the float in place. Swaying in the water, Brenda Louise balanced on the rope like a circus acrobat.

"Rosie, grab the rope."

Rosie's head popped out of the water. She stood on the rope next to Brenda Louise. Water dripped off her nose. They both turned toward the shore. They heard shouts and barking.

"What's going on?" Rosie asked.

Brenda Louise shaded her eyes, looking back toward the beach. What a commotion! Mr. Brown ran up and down the shore with a crowd of people running after him. He barked and dashed in and out of the water. Rosie and Brenda Louise looked at each other. They'd forgotten about Mr. Brown!

"Oh, no," said Rosie. She stood on her tiptoes, swaying back and forth. "They'll catch him. Poor Mr. Brown!"

But Mr. Brown ran into the water and started swimming straight for them.

"McClure!" Brenda Louise yelled, and turned toward the float.

McClure stood on the edge of the float with a bunch of kids, her hands shielding her eyes. "It's okay. He's a good swimmer." She did a racing dive, spanking the water flat out. The kids stood there, watching her.

"Wow," Brenda Louise said. "She sure can swim."

Rosie nodded. "So can Mr. Brown."

It was true. Mr. Brown paddled quickly. They waited for him to reach the rope. He swam up to Brenda Louise, licking her face and splashing. His paws scratched as he wiggled.

"Oh, Mr. Brown," Brenda Louise said, and buried her head in his wet fur. "You're a loyal friend." She kept falling off the rope as he wiggled against her in the water.

"He's a true Flying Chicken," McClure added as she swam to them.

"Yeah," Rosie said. "But how are we going to get him up on the float?"

Brenda Louise looked at the float. Mr. Brown was big. A wet dog would be heavy. It was hard enough to get themselves up there.

"We'll need help. I can ask the kids on the float." McClure swam over to the ladder and climbed onto the float.

There weren't too many kids there, but Brenda Louise recognized Rusty Gibbons and Jimmie Scanlon. McClure was in for it. Brenda Louise pushed away from the rope with her feet so she could watch McClure. The last time Rusty

Gibbons had seen Brenda Louise by the float, he'd done a cannonball and had almost sunk her. And, of course, the last time they'd met at her house, he'd bombarded her with water bombs.

"She'll never get help," Rosie told Brenda Louise. "Not with those two creeps."

Brenda Louise watched as McClure squeezed the water out of her hair. Her blue suit looked shiny and sleek in the sun. Brenda Louise heard her crazy laugh, heard Rusty doing his imitation of Donald Duck. It wouldn't be long before he'd see Rosie and Brenda Louise. He'd probably do something mean. Brenda Louise moved back to be close to the float. Rosie and Mr. Brown were already there, hiding in the shadows. No one standing on top would be able to see them now.

Mr. Brown put his paws on Brenda Louise's shoulders to lick her face. Her arms were getting scratched from his nails. His paw caught on her suit.

"Hi, Brenda Louise." Rusty leaned over the float, his face upside down as he looked at them.

"Hi, yourself," Brenda Louise told him.

"You and Rosie need to get the dog over by the ladder. We're going to hoist him up."

Rosie and Brenda Louise looked at each other. "You're going to help us?" She couldn't believe it.

Rusty grinned upside down. "You'll need to

guide him. You two can give him a boost once we get hold of him. McClure'll dive under and push him out of the water."

"Now, how can she do that?" Rosie asked. "Mr. Brown's a big dog. He's heavy."

"Is this for real?" Brenda Louise asked.

"Trust us," Rusty said. His face was in the shadow from the float, so you couldn't see all his freckles. Brenda Louise almost believed him.

Brenda Louise and Rosie inched themselves over to the ladder, careful not to move too far away from the cover and safety of the side. Rusty might look sincere, but he'd probably do something rotten. Everyone but McClure knew that.

McClure dived into the water and surfaced. "Let me know when I should dive down to boost Mr. Brown up," she told Brenda Louise.

"Don't be in such a rush," Rosie complained. She linked one arm on the ladder railing and crouched on the bottom rung.

Mr. Brown and Brenda Louise moved close to the ladder. Rusty and Jimmie lay on their stomachs, the tops of their bodies draped over the float.

"This is crazy," Brenda Louise said. "Just wait till they find out how heavy Mr. Brown is."

"Brenda Louise, are you going to direct this thing or not?" Rusty glared at her.

"Okay, McClure—dive!"

She did a surface dive. Brenda Louise could see

a dark shape under the water and a trail of bubbles. Suddenly, Mr. Brown looked really surprised. One ear went straight up in the air. The other ear was half bent. His body shot out of the water and then gently slid back in.

McClure surfaced. She sputtered and laughed. "I'll try again." She kicked her feet and floated.

Brenda Louise waited for Rusty to make one of his mean jokes.

"Go for it," Rusty said to McClure.

Brenda Louise looked at him, amazed. Maybe he'd been in the sun too long.

"Dive," Brenda Louise told McClure.

Down she shot again. This time Mr. Brown hovered higher in the water. The boys leaned over the top of the float and grabbed him. For a second, he hung in the air. It was just Mr. Brown, Rusty, and Jimmie. The boys grunted. They muttered. But they lifted Mr. Brown up higher and braced themselves against his weight.

Mr. Brown slipped. The boys bent over even further. Brenda Louise linked her arm on the ladder and helped support Mr. Brown. Mr. Brown pawed the air.

"It's okay," Brenda Louise told Mr. Brown. He looked so sad. There was a long, thin piece of what looked like seaweed caught between his nails.

"Come on, easy, boy." Rusty shifted. His muscles strained against the weight of Mr. Brown.

Brenda Louise had never even noticed he had muscles.

Rosie moved up the ladder, under Mr. Brown, pushing.

Mr. Brown struggled out of Rusty's arms and scrambled onto the flat surface of the float. Brenda Louise heard his nails clicking. The seaweed kept moving up the ladder after him.

"We did it," Rusty yelled.

Rosie danced up the ladder and onto the float next to Mr. Brown. McClure clapped her hands as she floated in the water. Brenda Louise started to climb up the ladder, too. There was a piece of what she thought was more seaweed hanging from her suit, dangling against her leg. It fell apart, slipping out of her hand. It was a thread from something. And that's when she realized. . . .

Her bathing suit was unraveling.

Brenda Louise stood on the ladder. Carefully, she felt the back of her suit. Below her shoulders, where the material used to meet the straps, she felt bare skin.

She sank back into the water without making a ripple. She took a deep breath. Her fingers edged down the front. More skin. Bare skin. She squinted up at the float and quickly turned around to face the beach.

"Hurry up, Brenda Louise, you're taking forever," Rusty complained. "We're going to play follow the leader off the diving board."

As Brenda Louise turned toward him, Rusty did a cartwheel across the top of the float. "Come on up," he said when he stood upright again.

"I'm going back to the beach," Brenda Louise said. By now, she was afraid to breathe too deeply or move too fast. Underwater, her hands moved down her chest. Finally she found bathing-suit material. Whew. She took a deep breath. Then she felt another row of stitching pop.

Her face felt hot, bright red, even in the cold water.

"What's this about you going in?" Rosie asked. "We just got here. The board isn't that high, Brenda Louise. Don't be chicken." Rosie leaned over and picked something off the top of the float. "What's the strap to your bathing suit doing up here?"

"It can't be my strap."

"Oh, yeah?" She looked at Brenda Louise suspiciously. "Then why aren't you coming up on the float?"

"Mind your own business." Her heart pounding, Brenda Louise treaded water backward as she talked, moving away as fast as she dared.

Rusty and Jimmie ran to the edge and peered over the water at her. Rusty grinned. "I have to go in, too." He elbowed Jimmie. They both laughed. "Wait up, Brenda Louise."

"You keep away from me, Rusty Gibbons!"

Brenda Louise shrieked. She kicked her legs hard to get away. Her legs felt free in the water. Then she realized why. The whole bottom of her bathing suit had fallen off. *No!* It couldn't be true. *Her whole bathing suit!* She wanted to sink. Her heart pounded. She turned around, frantic. Could anybody see?

What if Rusty swam close enough to see! She'd kick him, that's what.

Rusty laughed again and jumped into the water with a big splash. Brenda Louise gritted her teeth. She'd get Rosie. And Rusty, too.

"You're all horrible!" she yelled, and swam as fast as she could toward shore.

"What happened?" McClure yelled, swimming up beside her.

Brenda Louise gulped air and salt water together. "It's all gone—*my whole suit!*" She started swimming toward shore again. She felt herself shaking, and not just from the cold water.

When Brenda Louise turned her head, she saw Rusty swimming straight toward her. "McClure!" Brenda Louise yelled.

"I'm right here," McClure answered. She was swimming parallel. "I'll get you a towel."

It seemed to take forever to swim to shore. Brenda Louise swam as fast as she could. Through a saltwater blur, she saw McClure swim ahead, then run up the beach. She grabbed a towel off the sand and ran back into the water toward Brenda Louise.

"Here." McClure threw the towel out to her.

But the towel floated on top of the water, just out of reach. Rusty made a flying leap, trying to get it, but Brenda Louise lurched forward and grabbed the edge. She could just touch bottom.

"I *hate* you, Rusty Gibbons!" she shrieked.

She wrapped the towel around her middle. It wasn't big enough to cover her top. With one hand, Brenda Louise clutched the towel, tightly wrapped around her bottom. She held her other arm over her chest. Crouching low, she ran.

"Stop her!" A lady was running after her. "She has my towel!"

Brenda Louise heard laughter. A man said, "Lady, she needs it more than you do."

Out of the water and onto the hot sand she flew. Through tears, she saw color, people, and sand melt away. Brenda Louise ran and ran. Her feet pounded the boardwalk. She could hear her breath, hoarse and deep. Her heart thumped.

Down the maze of boardwalk paths she ran, gasping for breath. There was a pain in her side. She kicked the bathhouse door open. Inside, it was dark. She slammed the door shut. She stood shaking, her teeth chattered.

Summer was ruined.

Her life was ruined.

She leaned against the wall. From outside, she heard the sound of running feet, then pounding on the door. "Brenda Louise!" She looked out the air slats. It was McClure and Rosie. Traitor Rosie.

"Go away."

"It wasn't as bad as you think," McClure said.

"It's not like you have anything to show," Rosie added, "that anyone would care to see."

A lot she knew. She didn't have to announce it to the world.

"On the Riviera, French ladies go topless all the time," McClure said.

"They do?" Rosie and Brenda Louise asked together.

"Of course," said McClure.

"Even you?" Brenda Louise asked.

"What do you think?" McClure laughed. It was a laugh that let Brenda Louise know that it wasn't any big deal—not to the French, anyway.

It was a big deal here, though.

Brenda Louise heard Mr. Brown sniffing at the door, scratching, trying to get in.

"Look," Rosie said, "Granny's going to be furious because I've been gone so long. I've gotta go help. The line's too long at the snack bar." Rosie turned to go. "I'm sorry, Brenda Louise, for being a jerk out at the float."

"Well, you were," Brenda Louise said. She opened the door a crack. She took a deep breath.

"You guys *really* don't think it was too bad? I mean, I was *naked.*"

"So, big deal." Rosie ran down the boardwalk.

"Hardly anyone noticed," McClure told her. "Well, that's not exactly true. The lady who owns that beach towel sure noticed."

"Oh, McClure, it was so awful." Ordinarily, Brenda Louise opened the door wider and dressed in the light from outside. This time, she dressed in the dark. She pulled her pink T-shirt on over her shorts. Then she opened the door and peeked out. "McClure, can I borrow your big sunglasses? I'll wear Mom's beach hat, too. I can't face everybody."

McClure handed Brenda Louise her sunglasses. "Let's go help Rosie down at the snack bar. Then you won't have to think about it."

"Are you crazy? All I want to do is hide. I was stark naked!" Suddenly, it seemed funny. Brenda Louise started to laugh, but her laughing stopped as she remembered. Mortified. She'd been mortified. She'd felt wobbly-kneed, like a jellyfish. She wasn't sure if she should laugh or cry.

"I didn't know you could swim that fast," McClure said, grinning. "You'd be pretty good if you'd go in a straight line."

Brenda Louise looked over the top of the sunglasses at McClure. "I didn't have a swimsuit to slow me down."

"Brenda Louise, hardly anybody saw who it was. Just keep the sunglasses on. Nobody will know."

"If they didn't see, why do I need the sunglasses?" Brenda Louise felt Mr. Brown's cool nose sniffing her feet. She crouched down on the boardwalk and hugged him.

"You don't need them. *Suivez-moi!* Follow me," McClure said. Brenda Louise stood up. Mr. Brown pranced beside her on the boardwalk.

"Rosie needs us. Look at that long line at the snack bar," McClure said. She saluted Brenda Louise and started to march down the boardwalk. Brenda Louise pulled the brim of Mom's beach hat low. She glanced around the beach. No one was looking! She marched after McClure and Mr. Brown, stomping her feet as she went.

When they arrived at the snack bar, they went right up to the counter. "We're here to help," Brenda Louise said to Rosie.

Granny looked at them with her eyebrows raised and her lips pursed. "Double trouble just arrived."

Rosie flipped hamburgers, adding pickle relish to the meat—cooking gourmet. McClure handed out soda pop from the cooler.

Granny sank into her chair and shook her head. Brenda Louise took her place at the counter and handed out food. Sometimes she even wiped the countertop. She kept her sunglasses on. At the same time, she looked out at the shimmering water, daydreaming. Before long, the line disappeared.

Rosie scooped ice cream, nice big scoops of chocolate perched on top of a sugar cone. She handed it to Brenda Louise.

"Thanks for helping, Brenda Louise."

She didn't say "Metal Mouth." Sometimes Rosie was okay.

Brenda Louise licked the ice cream, chasing the melted drops with her tongue. Rosie packed another cone high with scoops of chocolate and handed it to McClure.

"Look who's coming," Rosie whispered.

Brenda Louise leaned over the counter and watched Rusty and Jimmie walk toward the snack bar. She felt heat creep up her neck.

Rusty stood right in front of her. He shuffled his bare feet. He looked embarrassed. "We want two chocolate ice-cream cones." Rusty looked miserable. "And, um, I'm sorry about what happened, Brenda Louise."

"It's okay," Brenda Louise said. But it wasn't.

Her hand shook as she made their ice-cream cones. Rusty'd been so mean. Suddenly the whole scene flashed before her again.

The ice cream dribbled down on her hand. The horrible memory disappeared. She stared at Rusty from across the counter. "You get free sprinkles." She spoke low so Granny wouldn't hear.

Under the counter, Brenda Louise dipped the cones in salt, then a layer of chocolate sprinkles. She smiled and handed them the cones. "No hard feelings, huh? See ya."

Quickly, the girls lowered the outside awning. But Brenda Louise watched Rusty and Jimmie as they walked along the boardwalk, licking their ice-cream cones. She had a funny feeling, like maybe she'd gone too far. Maybe he was sincere this time. Nope! He'd been rotten. He deserved it.

The boys kept walking down the boardwalk. Maybe she hadn't put enough salt on the cones. Suddenly Rusty threw his cone into the sand below. He turned and glared. Brenda Louise jumped back so that he wouldn't see her watching.

"Brenda Louise, it's okay. They've gone. And we've gotta go home. Grab the jacket, okay?" Brenda Louise lifted the aviator jacket up and inhaled. It smelled of pickles and salt air—like a snack bar—just as Granny had predicted.

"It's a matter of character. A jacket has to age," McClure said.

Brenda Louise agreed. She scooped up her sneakers and hung them around her neck.

Mr. Brown shook sand off his coat and trotted along with them.

"See ya, Rosie," Brenda Louise and McClure yelled as they left the beach.

McClure looked at Brenda Louise as they walked."You know, I've been writing letters to my parents." She held her knapsack by the straps. It bumped her legs as they walked. "I didn't get a chance to say anything before, with all the bathing suit trouble."

Brenda Louise stopped. "Any luck?" She held her breath.

"Yes. I got a letter." She pulled a paper out of her knapsack, skimmed the writing, and then read aloud.

" 'We loved your letters. We were surprised to receive a packet from the Paradise Lane Neighborhood Association. And we were pleased to receive the church bulletin and see your name in it. We'll be coming to Hill House soon.' "

McClure folded the letter and put it back into her knapsack. "At least they know I'm really doing okay. Who knows—maybe it'll do some good."

"Of course it will!"

They shuffled along, their heads down, past the tennis courts. Brenda Louise kept her face turned away so she wouldn't have to see. Nicky would take care of her racket. Everything would be okay.

It had been a week since McClure had heard from her parents. Brenda Louise's mom still dropped Brenda Louise off at tennis class every morning. And Brenda Louise no longer felt self-conscious about using Mom's old racket. It was true—no one else had a racket like it. But the more Brenda Louise played tennis, the more she saw how good Mom's racket really was. So when she remembered, after class, she would slip the head into a plastic sleeve and use a wooden press to keep the frame from warping.

"Someone challenged you to a match next

week," Nicky said as he walked with Brenda Louise across the court.

"Who'd do that?" She didn't know enough to play a challenge match.

"Some kid signed up. You'll have to check the challenge sheet. I don't remember the name." Nicky shook his head. "But I do remember it's the same time I have a private lesson, nine o'clock, on Wednesday. Next week, hotshot." Nicky looked at Brenda Louise and smiled.

Brenda Louise walked to the other side of the court, bumping her racket against the toes of her sneakers. Who would challenge her? She reached the back of the court and faced Nicky, ready for practice shots.

"You've got a lot of work to do," Nicky said from across the net. He bounced a ball. With a graceful arc, he swung his racket. The ball sailed across the net.

And she thought Kimberley made her run! She ran all over the court, panting, out of breath. It wasn't fair. He was the professional, and she was just a beginner. He wasn't letting her win any points at all. She got so mad, she aimed the ball at Nicky; whenever she hit him, she counted it as a point for herself.

"The idea, Brenda Louise, is to hit the balls so I can't hit them back—make me run *to* the ball, not away from it."

Okay. If that was the way he wanted it. Brenda Louise spun the ball, dropped it over the net, or placed it in the farthest corner of the court. Sweat ran down her face, the salt stinging her eyes. She squinted at Nicky. Her mind raced. If she bounced the ball real high, it would slow him down. She felt mean.

Nicky walked over to the net. He'd yell at her. She didn't care anymore. It was a dumb game.

"Great. You're ready." He smiled. "What a natural. No wonder your mother wants you to play. I used to watch her play here. She was one of the best."

"You aren't mad? All those things I did?" She couldn't believe it. He still liked her.

"I wouldn't try target practice again. But the rest—it was good tennis."

"Are you sure you don't know who challenged me?" Brenda Louise asked, suddenly suspicious. Rosie? No. Rosie was too good.

Nicky rubbed his leg where one of the tennis balls she hit had smacked him. "Beats me. Just be here Wednesday."

Rosie met her as she walked off the court. "That was real original, Brenda Louise. Never saw anything quite like it."

"Somebody challenged me to a match."

"Who in the world would do that?" Rosie asked.

"I don't know," Brenda Louise bristled. "It's going to be on Wednesday. I need all the support I can get."

"I wouldn't miss it," Rosie said.

"After the game, we can have a meeting of the Flying Chickens," Brenda Louise said, her voice softer as she looked out at the ocean. "I've got a new bathing suit, and it should be high tide. Just right for flying off the diving board."

"If your suit stays together, we should be fine." Rosie ran along the fence toward the snack bar. "See you."

Of course, her suit would stay together. It was brand-new. She wouldn't ever wear an old bathing suit again. Never ever. And she didn't want to think about that day anymore.

She had to get home, call McClure, and ask her to watch the tennis match and go flying next week. Brenda Louise was suddenly suspicious. Could it be McClure who had challenged her? McClure had a new racket; Brenda Louise had seen it in her room at Hill House.

As soon as Brenda Louise got home, she dialed McClure's telephone number.

"Hello," McClure said on the other end.

"Someone challenged me to a tennis match! Next Wednesday." In her excitement, Brenda Louise blurted the words out.

"I thought you hated tennis," McClure said.

"Well, I do, but now I can hit the ball." When had she started to like tennis? Brenda Louise was amazed.

There was so much noise at McClure's end that Brenda Louise could hardly hear her. "Come on up," McClure yelled into the receiver.

"I will," Brenda Louise yelled back. McClure didn't seem very excited about her news.

Brenda Louise trudged up the hill. McClure could've been just a little bit impressed. After all, Brenda Louise had been hitting that old backboard for weeks. And volleying with Kimberley. It was about time she made progress. If it was McClure who'd challenged, she sure was being sneaky about it.

As Brenda Louise walked up the gravel drive, she passed cars and trucks parked on either side, all the way up to Hill House. Her sneakers made a crunchy sound on the gravel. Workers were everywhere. What was going on?

At Hill House, she yelled through the open door, over the sounds of pounding and sawing, "McClure, McClure!" McClure didn't answer. Brenda Louise ran around to the back. They must be mending Hill House, cleaning things up.

She found McClure by the old pool. "I've looked everywhere for you," Brenda Louise complained. "What's going on around here?"

"I told you. My parents are coming. My uncle is fixing the place up."

"When do they come?"

"Next weekend. There's going to be a big bash. We're getting everything ready."

Brenda Louise's insides turned upside down. Her speech for McClure's parents! What would she tell them? She hadn't expected to have to do it so soon. She wasn't ready. Well, she'd have to think of something.

Brenda Louise looked around. She sort of liked the wildness of Hill House. It had been tangled and overgrown when McClure was away. Now it was going to look like everyplace else with manicured lawns and vacuumed drives. All the wildness gone, wiped clear.

"They're going to clean this old swimming pool," McClure said.

They stood on the edge of the pool, looking into green slime. Mr. Brown stepped down the stairs and into the water, making a pathway as he swam.

McClure knelt and trailed her hand in the water. She jumped back as Mr. Brown got out of the pool and shook green slime drops all over her. McClure wiped her arms. She was speckled all over with tiny green spots.

Brenda Louise looked down at her own clothes. Oh, no! There was a streak of green slime on *her*

T-shirt. She rubbed the spot. Only the more she rubbed, the bigger it got. Brenda Louise knelt by the pool and splashed water on her shirt. "I don't think it'll ever come out," she said.

McClure hopped around to her side. "So we're speckled. Look." She rubbed the slime away off the side of the pool. "Look at the tile. Blue and green. It's beautiful."

But the pool stank. A wet Mr. Brown snuggled next to Brenda Louise. She held her nose. "Phew! Get away!" Mr. Brown's tail drooped. "Aw, come here." Brenda Louise scratched behind his ears.

She imagined how the clean pool would look. It would be fun. On a hot fall day, they could walk up the hill after school, jump in, and cool off.

"Come on," McClure said. They ran down the path, with Mr. Brown dashing after them, barking.

There were big heaps of ivy and blackberry brambles on the walkway. "They're cleaning the whole place out. They uncovered the old tennis court." McClure pointed through the trees.

She ran down the hill out onto the clay surface. "Well, what do you think?" She twirled around, obviously pleased.

"About what?"

"The court. I've weeded all week. While you've been in tennis class, I've been working here. It's my project, my surprise."

As far as Brenda Louise could see, the court needed at least two more weeks of weeding. But she couldn't tell McClure. McClure was all happy and dancing around.

"I know it needs a lot more." McClure pointed to the net, which sagged in the middle and dragged on the ground. "It looks pretty sad, even cleaned up."

"I wonder when anyone played here last." Brenda Louise walked out onto the uneven clay. It had the feel of mystery about it. She wondered if Mom and McClure's mother had played there long ago.

"I was hoping you'd help me," McClure answered. "Roll the court and paint lines."

Inside, Brenda Louise groaned. She was *so* tired. Working in the hot sun was the last thing she wanted to do. But McClure was her friend. Brenda Louise rolled up her sleeves. "Okay. Let's get busy."

McClure dragged the hose as Brenda Louise ran back and turned on the water. They filled the roller drum. It took both of them to push it across the clay. They worked for an hour. They did it over and over. Brenda Louise rubbed her forehead, dizzy in the sun.

"Don't you think we've done enough? We've been out here forever."

"Okay. I think it's flatter. We've put in a lot of work," McClure said.

"Can you come watch my match Wednesday?" Brenda Louise watched McClure, trying to see if she was the secret challenger.

"Sure," McClure said. She looked completely innocent.

"We can have a meeting of the Flying Chickens, too. I already asked Rosie." Brenda Louise studied McClure, wondering.

"Great. Look how nice everything looks." McClure stood on the side of the court. Brenda Louise shaded her eyes with her arm. The court did look better.

"We need something cool to drink. How about some lemonade? There's a jug in the kitchen. I'll get it. Meet me in the toolshed."

"That's the best idea you've had this afternoon." Brenda Louise ran down to the shed. It was always cool and quiet inside. The stone walls blocked outside noise. The door was padlocked, but the window lock was broken. She lifted the window up and slipped in, then held the window open for Mr. Brown. He jumped in. The grape arbor outside filtered the sunlight like a pale green, leafy canopy. The green light made Brenda Louise feel like she was in a forest.

She crouched on the dirt floor as a figure passed

by the front windows. There was a musty, earthen smell.

"Brenda Louise," McClure whispered. She held the window open. "Here's the lemonade."

"You were quick," Brenda Louise whispered back. She held the jug as McClure slid into the shed. McClure lifted old jelly glasses off the windowsill and polished them with her shirt. "Here, pour the lemonade. We'll toast to your tennis match Wednesday."

"Okay," Brenda Louise said. "And to another meeting of the Flying Chickens."

They sat down on the floor, put their feet up on bushel baskets, and lifted their jelly glasses in the air. They clinked their glasses together. Mr. Brown lay next to them, wagging his tail.

"And, most important," Brenda Louise added, "to convincing your parents to let you stay on Paradise Lane."

McClure grinned. *"Bien sûr!* Of course!"

They held the jelly glasses high. The light from outside made little rainbows on the wall.

19

The night before her tennis match, Brenda Louise couldn't sleep. All night she tossed. Her feet tangled in the sheets. First, she dreamed of tennis. Just as she was about to see who had challenged her, she woke up. Then, when she finally went back to sleep, she dreamed about McClure's parents and the party. In her dream, she chased them with a tennis racket and yelled, "Let McClure stay!"

It was a relief to finally wake up and find sunshine streaming through the window, to hear birds singing outside. Her tennis racket lay against the chair, where she'd left it. Next to it, rolled up in a towel, was the new fire-engine red bathing suit Mom had bought her. The red material peeked out from the roll.

Brenda Louise jumped up, stretched, and took a deep breath. Today was the big day. She grabbed a white shirt and shorts. In two minutes she was dressed. Mom drove her to the tennis courts, stopping first to pick up McClure and Mr. Brown.

"I'm wearing my bathing suit, so we can swim after your match," said McClure.

Brenda Louise clutched the rolled towel with her new suit wrapped up inside. "It'll feel good to get in the water." She opened the car window. Her hair blew in the wind. "I hope I play okay."

She'd gone to the tennis hut to see the sign-up board. Her name was there, all right. And if she won, she'd be on the challenge board, with a chance to climb the tennis ladder. But someone had erased the name of whoever it was who had challenged her. Or maybe it had been smudged off when somebody leaned against the board.

"You'll have fun," McClure said.

Fun? It had never occurred to Brenda Louise to call this disaster *fun*. She hugged Mr. Brown. He rode with his head out the window, his ears flying. He wouldn't care if she won or lost.

They got to the tennis court early. Rosie sat

waiting, at the top of the bleachers, chewing a big wad of pink bubble gum. "I've got a can of new tennis balls for you, Metal Mouth. Only one missing."

"Thanks, Rosie." Brenda Louise wiped her hands on her shorts.

McClure climbed the bleachers to sit with Rosie. Mom took a seat right in front. Mr. Brown lay under the benches in the shade. Nicky waved from another court, where he was giving a private lesson.

Brenda Louise twisted her shirttail until it got all wrinkled.

"Is this the big match?" Kimberley asked as she walked up.

Brenda Louise exchanged a look of dread with McClure and Rosie. It couldn't be Kimberley! No way.

"Yes, this is the big match." Brenda Louise's voice dared Kimberley to say more.

"I'm going to watch. I can't believe you actually accepted a challenge when you don't know how to play."

"Well, I didn't know I was allowed to refuse." Brenda Louise was so relieved that it wasn't Kimberley who had challenged her that she forgot to be nervous. She balanced the end of her racket on her palm.

Rusty and Jimmie sauntered past. She turned away. That was all she needed. It was bad enough having Kimberley watch her game.

"Let's go," Rusty said.

"What do you mean?"

"We've got a game. I challenged you."

Brenda Louise dropped her racket. "You?"

"Yup." Rusty laughed.

From high up, she heard Rosie's bubble gum pop. Kimberley giggled.

"Okay." Brenda Louise fought to keep her voice level. She remembered the ice-cream cones she'd salted; and now here was Rusty, getting his revenge.

They walked out onto the court.

"I don't know how to serve. I haven't learned yet," Brenda Louise said.

"Just hit the ball to the right section of the court. We'll count it as a serve," Rusty said.

Brenda Louise bounced the ball and hit it. It plopped over the net. Rusty slammed it back. The ball zinged by her feet. Rusty hit hard.

His serves smashed into her court. She watched them whiz by. Sometimes she dodged them.

Her pretend serves were Marshmallow Fluff. He slaughtered them. All the while, he grinned at her from across the court. They changed sides, and he grinned. Since he made all the points, all the applause was for him.

But Brenda Louise was getting mad. Tennis was a mean game. On the outside, everyone was polite. On the inside, everyone plotted ways to destroy the other player. Rusty was good and fast and mean. He was out to get her. Well, he'd be surprised. She couldn't return his serves, but she could volley.

It was like she was at the backboard again. The next time Rusty hit the ball, Brenda Louise hit it back strong and clean. *Slam.* She shot the ball to the opposite court, away from Rusty. He had to run. Brenda Louise kept hitting and running. She never took her eye off the ball.

Sometimes, in the distance, she heard Rosie and McClure and Mom cheer. At least that was what it sounded like, in the heat of the game. There were times when she didn't think the whole thing would ever end.

But she started to earn points. Not many, but some. She studied the way Rusty hit. She ran after the long shots and charged the net. It was fun figuring out where to be next. It didn't matter that Rusty was better. She was playing the best she could. And she had discovered Rusty's weak stroke. She pounded away at his backhand.

Rusty mopped his forehead and stared across the court at her. He wasn't grinning anymore. Brenda Louise was making him run. But it wasn't enough. When she charged the net, he lobbed the ball. It sailed into the court behind her.

And he won.

Brenda Louise mopped her face with a towel. "Well, you beat me. That's what you wanted, isn't it?" She shook his hand the way she'd been taught. Tennis etiquette. She wanted to step on his foot.

"Good game, Brenda Louise."

"You smeared me."

"Yup. But you held your own."

He was right about that.

"We should play doubles sometime. Maybe against McClure and Jimmie. Or Rosie and someone." Rusty smiled at her.

Brenda Louise had never noticed his eyes before. Blue like the sky. And his crooked grin. "Thanks for the game." She floated off the court and over to the bleachers. Wow.

"You gave my old racket quite a workout," Mom smiled.

"It's a good racket, Mom."

"I'll be over there." Mom pointed to the chairs under the trees. "I brought a book to read."

"Don't feel bad, Brenda Louise. You played okay," McClure told her.

"We've gotta work on your serve," Rosie said as she slid down from the bleachers.

Kimberley stood up. "It was the worst match I've ever seen. How can you tell her she did okay? She missed even the *easy* shots. I'm surprised someone as good as Rusty Gibbons asked you to play."

"Me, too." Brenda Louise giggled. She gave McClure and Rosie a thumbs-up. McClure snapped her fingers, and Mr. Brown wiggled out from under the bleachers. The four of them walked together toward the beach.

"He wants to play again, maybe doubles." Brenda Louise spun around in a circle.

Rosie and McClure nudged each other and giggled. Rosie wiggled her eyebrows.

"Brenda Louise likes Rusty," she sang out in a falsetto voice.

"Shh," Brenda Louise said. "Someone'll hear." She looked around the beach. Before them, the ocean sparkled. Little whitecaps topped the waves.

"This time, I'm leaving Mr. Brown on the beach." McClure pulled her T-shirt off. "Brenda Louise, if you open your eyes when you swim, you'll go straight." She pulled off her shorts and stood before them in her blue French bathing suit.

"I'll meet you guys out at the float." Brenda Louise turned toward the bathhouse.

"With a bathing suit, I hope," said Rosie.

"Just you wait." Brenda Louise ran to the bathhouse and put on her new suit. It was beautiful. She took a deep breath and walked out onto the beach. McClure and Rosie stood on the float waving at her. She ran into the water and kept her eyes open as she swam. She swam straight.

"Great!" McClure yelled when Brenda Louise finally reached the ladder on the float.

"My eyes are full of salt water." Brenda Louise pulled herself up the ladder.

Music from someone's boat floated over the water. One by one, single file, they danced out onto the diving board, bending and turning to the beat. Brenda Louise's new swimsuit glistened in the sun.

"Flying Chickens!" Brenda Louise yelled. They leaped in the sun, into the sky. The air whistled around them and they splashed down, plunging into the sparkling water below.

20

The day of the big bash for McClure's parents, Brenda Louise washed her hair with Mom's shampoo. It was supposed to make hair shiny. By the time she got to the driveway of McClure's house, her hair was dry and the whole top of her dress had a damp ring around the collar. But the shampoo had worked. Her hair was shiny bright. She felt ready to see McClure's parents.

Brenda Louise's mom and dad walked ahead, while Tom walked alongside her. "Your dress is soaked," he said.

"It'll dry." Brenda Louise shook her hair in the

afternoon sun. To herself, she rehearsed what she planned to say to McClure's parents. The wording would be important. But it was hard to concentrate. She was too excited.

When they got to Hill House, McClure opened the door for them. She wore a long skirt like a sarong, looking all grown up. Rosie had on a hot-pink dress. She'd combed all her hair on top of her head. McClure and Rosie looked older. Brenda Louise wished she looked older, too. Maybe if she wore her hair up. Next time, she'd try it.

McClure asked her to help pass things, which was good because it made her forget how she felt. They passed little silver bowls filled with tiny chocolates.

People kept talking, nibbling the chocolates as they visited. McClure, Brenda Louise, and Rosie moved around the room and outside on the terrace, listening to the grown-up talk.

"The chocolate is excellent. French?" A lady wearing a polka-dot dress smiled at McClure. She reached for another handful.

McClure nodded. "Or Swiss; I'm not sure. The ants are from Africa. I am sure about that."

The woman paused, her hand hovering over the bowl. "Ants. How interesting." Her face drained of color. "Excuse me, dear."

"Of course," said McClure. She wiggled one eyebrow at Brenda Louise as the lady hurried away.

Brenda Louise smothered her giggles and wiggled one eyebrow back. She'd practiced all month to do that.

Rosie collapsed in a chair, laughing. "That was great!" Strands of her hair fell from the top of her head. She looked more like Rosie again.

Brenda Louise watched McClure's parents. They didn't seem to notice McClure. Everywhere they went, there was a crowd, lights, wires, and cameras. Then, as Brenda Louise turned to the buffet, McClure's mother walked over.

"Darling, just a few pictures," she said to McClure.

McClure's mother was beautiful. She looked young and skinny. Her dress floated like transparent, shimmering rainbows. McClure's dad joined her. He towered over them like a big bear. The three of them posed in the sunlight on the terrace, standing close together.

Brenda Louise imagined the caption on the photograph: "T. J. and Sam Wallingford with their daughter, McClure, at their country home on Paradise Lane."

"Brenda Louise! Rosie!" McClure called out. "Come see my mom and dad." She turned toward them. "You remember Brenda Louise," McClure said as Brenda Louise walked up. "And this is Rosie. They're my friends." The way she said it made Brenda Louise feel special.

Brenda Louise mumbled "Hi" and looked down. Good grief. What would she say to them?

McClure kept talking, bubbling over with excitement. "Would someone take pictures?" She elbowed Brenda Louise and whispered, "For the Flying Chickens."

Brenda Louise felt her braces with her tongue. She had to remember not to smile.

While the photographer set up again, McClure ran off. She came back, out of breath, wearing her genuine leather World War II aviator jacket. Brenda Louise gave her a thumbs-up. Suddenly, she didn't care if her braces showed or not. They were the Flying Chickens! Mr. Brown slouched against her right foot, scratching his tummy. Rosie blew a bubble with her gum; it flopped back and forth in the breeze. And that's when the photographer took the picture.

"Come on," McClure whispered, and shoved Brenda Louise in front of her parents. "Now's your chance. Make it good. You've got to convince them."

Brenda Louise cleared her throat and took a deep breath. "I think I have laryngitis."

McClure's parents leaned closer, watching Brenda Louise carefully. Her hands were clammy. "We need McClure," she began. "We need her to stay."

McClure nodded in agreement. Her parents beamed. They were supposed to be upset. Instead, they looked like parents do when they try to encourage kids to give a good speech at the school assembly.

"She's my friend." Brenda Louise's voice boomed out, having suddenly returned in full volume. Its loudness surprised her. But McClure's parents just nodded, smiling.

"We've got a good school right here. It isn't fancy like that school in Switzerland. But it's good." Brenda Louise gave them her fierce look, daring them to challenge her.

"The basketball team stinks," Rosie interrupted.

"But the school is good," Brenda Louise continued. "Everybody turns out okay." She stared at McClure's parents. McClure's mom had green eyes, just like McClure's.

"Please let her stay for school this year." There, she'd said it.

She heard a deep, deep voice. It was McClure's dad. "It isn't easy to do what you ask, Brenda Louise. But we'll give it every consideration."

"Oh, I've got more. We've talked it over. Rosie, McClure, and me. We can all help out with money, too."

McClure's father looked surprised. "How would

you do that, Brenda Louise?" He bent down and looked at her closely.

"We don't have the details worked out yet." She took a deep breath and plunged on. "But we could do things like helping Tom with his newspaper route and baby-sitting and mowing lawns. And weeding. Caring for tennis courts." That last one was a good idea. Brenda Louise was pleased she had thought of it.

"I see." He nodded.

"And that's not all!"

"No, I guess it wouldn't be," McClure's dad said.

"We're going to be part of the tennis team. Our school's famous for its tennis program. European school wouldn't have that. Not like it is here."

McClure and Rosie looked surprised. Brenda Louise had to admit the tennis team was a good idea, too. It had a nice ring to it.

McClure's dad cleared his throat. "Brenda Louise, McClure is fortunate to have you as a friend. And Rosie, too." He smiled the way grownups do when they want to be kind.

Brenda Louise looked down at her feet. She twisted her fingers together, and her lower lip trembled. She stared at the floor.

McClure's mom wrapped Brenda Louise in her arms. "You sweet children. Charming." She lifted Brenda Louise's face upward. "Brenda Louise, you are beautiful." There was the smell of violets in

the air. Then McClure's parents were gone, sur-
rounded by people.

Sweet? Charming? Beautiful? Brenda Louise
smiled. She felt her braces with her tongue. Beautiful. Part of her felt like bursting. What a wonderful thing for McClure's mother to say. The other
part of her felt discouraged. She kept hearing
McClure's dad. She didn't think she'd convinced
him about McClure.

"He was too nice. It was probably a put-down, a
nice put-down," Rosie said.

"I guess I flubbed it." Brenda Louise bit her lip.

"No, you did a good job," McClure said.

Brenda Louise caught sight of her mom waving.
"I've gotta go." She sighed. "My parents are giving the signal like I better not waste time."

McClure slipped out of the jacket and handed it
to her. "Here, wear this home. I'll see you later. As
soon as the party's over."

"Okay!" Brenda Louise ran down the stone path
toward her parents. She put the jacket on. Why
should she think the worst? Maybe McClure would
be able to stay.

At home, all evening Brenda Louise kept looking
for McClure. She was tired. Mom told her to forget
it, to see McClure in the morning. Finally, Brenda
Louise lay down. But she left the window open

wide so that she'd hear if McClure came by out-side. Even so, Brenda Louise almost missed Mc-Clure altogether.

"Brenda Louise," a voice called out. "Wake up."

Brenda Louise woke up with a start. She felt a piece of gravel bounce off the sheet. There was gravel all over her bed. Someone was pelting her.

She leaped out of bed, dumping gravel and her sheets on the floor. In two jumps she was at the window. "McClure?" she whispered into the dark-ness.

She heard McClure's low laugh, heard Mr. Brown shake, jingling the tags on his collar. She grabbed the aviator jacket and climbed out the window to the apple tree. It was easy climbing down. She'd done it lots of times. She let go of the bottom branch and landed with a thump.

"Where are you?" she called in a loud whisper.

"Over here."

There, on top of the garage roof, next to the plum tree, sat McClure and Mr. Brown. Mr. Brown wig-gled all over, his nails going clickety-click on the roof as he greeted Brenda Louise. McClure rattled the gravel in her pockets.

"I needed a big supply to throw in your win-dow." She chuckled.

"What'd they say? Your parents, I mean. Will they let you stay?" Brenda Louise looked up at McClure and Mr. Brown on the roof.

McClure's hair shimmered in the moonlight. She sighed. "I have to go with them."

Brenda Louise had a dead weight inside where her heart was supposed to be.

"I don't want to go away," McClure said. Mr. Brown whimpered as though he understood.

"You can't go." Brenda Louise looked up at the garage roof. McClure and Mr. Brown blurred. She felt helpless. "When? When do you have to go?"

McClure spoke so softly that Brenda Louise almost didn't hear her. "Next weekend."

"Oh." There was nothing more to say.

"I need you to keep Mr. Brown. I can't just ask anyone. It has to be somebody special—someone I can trust."

"You mean it?" Brenda Louise asked. *Monsieur* Brown? A dog of her own? A dog on loan of her own? Her heart felt like it would burst.

"Well?" McClure asked.

"Sure," she said. Her voice squeaked. "You won't be sorry, McClure. Dad got me some language tapes. Why, I'll be speaking French before you know it. Mr. Brown will feel right at home. And I know Rosie will help, too."

"I knew I could count on you," McClure said. "You're just about the best friend anyone could ever have."

Brenda Louise grinned in the dark and hugged herself. Wishes *were* powerful. Especially wishes made at night, outside. "I wished for a best friend," she told McClure. "And you came home, and it all came true."

For a minute, everything was very quiet. She had her eyes shut so tight that she had to blink them open. "You'll be back before you know it."

McClure sighed again. Brenda Louise could see her shoulders slump. McClure might even have been crying.

Brenda Louise climbed the plum tree and scrambled onto the garage roof. She handed the jacket to McClure.

"You'll need this for your trip," she said, half hoping McClure would insist she keep it instead. But McClure took the jacket and slipped it on.

"Flying Chickens, prepare for night flight," McClure announced, her voice suddenly clear and even.

They stood on the safe side of the roof. Together Brenda Louise and McClure leaped into the black night. They floated in space, flying.